NOTHING SCARES ME

Gene Kemp

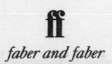

faber and faber

First published in 2006
by Faber and Faber Limited
3 Queen Square London WC1N 3AU

Printed in England by
Mackays of Chatham plc, Chatham, Kent

A CIP record for this book
is available from the British Library

ISBN 978-0-571-22823-2
ISBN 0-571-22823-2

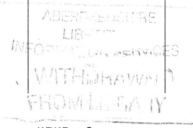
KEMP, Gene

Nothing scares me

by the same author

The Turbulent Term of Tyke Tiler
Charlie Lewis Plays for Time
Gowie Corby Plays Chicken
Zowie Corby's Story
Just Ferret
Juniper
Rebel Rebel
The Clock Tower Ghost
The Tyke Tiler Joke Book
Snaggletooth's Mystery
Seriously Weird

For Buffy, who saw it all:

From the outside, Compass Cottage is mysterious, magical. The overgrown garden still carries the essence of what it once was. Descending down into the wooded valley at the bottom of it small purple flowers peep through the weeds and brambles. But then returning along the path to the creaking front door you sense something else. And despite the family's cries of, 'Look at that. Isn't it beautiful?' I knew there was something badly wrong.

Peering through the windows, then trying the front door and entering into the empty, decrepit, diseased house I was overwhelmed by a feeling of dread. I acknowledged it but dismissed it. I wasn't going to believe what it was saying. But walking from room to room, seeing the dripping damp, cobwebby, fungus laden walls made me feel sick. You could smell the filth but this time in the atmosphere.

My sister Kate wanted to go up the rickety stairs, and I followed warily.

Then a powerful, forceful, aggressive shove hit me right in the ribs winding me, hurting.

I stopped. I had to get out of there. 'No,' I whispered to Kate, 'The stairs are too old.'

I went outside, stopped and breathed slowly. The pain went away.

But I knew something was in there. And the something knew me, too.

Slowly I walked to the barn behind the house. It had a tower on the top, a most extraordinary place. Inside the rubbish was piled high. Someone, something watched me from the corners. I ran out, along the drive and on to the grass verge beside the lane.

What was so wrong with Compass Cottage? What had happened there? Why the name? Was the encompassing thing there to protect, to stop things getting in, or to stop things getting out? Whatever, something existed in there, something that was . . . trapped.

Someone has now bought Compass Cottage and is planning to renovate and refurbish it, but no matter how hard they try, that being will still be there and they won't be refurbishing that house for long. No one will be able to help it or live there. Ever.

NOTHING SCARES ME

Some people have a 'sixth sense'. A feeling that wriggles around inside you when something's up that adds on to the other five senses. Other people wish to have one, only to control and understand maybe what they don't know. If you get one, you'll end up regretting that wish you made. Especially if it's anything like mine. This is the story of *my* sixth sense.

Only, it isn't all rainbow and candy-floss, or saving people from impending doom.

It is . . . NOTHING.

Petra Stevens

Chapter One

Sunday evening

> I met a boy upon a stair
> A little boy who wasn't there
> He wasn't there again today
> I wish he'd go away and stay –
> That's George

H-O-M-E-W-O-R-K. It shouldn't be allowed. It ought to be banned. For Ever. The curse of Children. Torture. Misery. Cruelty. HOMEWORK. Down with Homework. Burn it!!!!

I'd got five lots all to be given in tomorrow morning, and the words of a carol to be learnt. Yuck! Double yuck! I could've done it before but I always leave it till Sunday. Slowly I got stuck into making a list of Henry VIII's wives. Why couldn't he have just stuck to one? Why did he have to be so greedy? Why six? It was six, wasn't it? And I looked up to see George in his usual place, standing six inches off the floor by the big old bookcase. Granny (Mum's Mum) left it to us stuffed with old books, and George with them.

'Go away, George,' I hissed at him (I didn't want Mum hearing me. She says I make him up). 'Get lost. I've got tons of homework to do and some of it's late already. Go away. P-L-E-A-S-E.'

But he just stood there, grape-green eyes glaring at me, twiddling his nasty flat cap round in his hands, greeny-yellowy curls all over his head, bony wrists sticking out of his patched jacket, dirty short-longs or long-shorts reaching down to his scabby knees and the awful, awful huge Victorian Doc Marten boots with no laces in – his Dad's, I guess. He was no surprise. Like us, he lives here and he's about as scary as an old slice of bread. I'm really sorry for him. He must have led an awful life from the look of him. But I'd got to get on with my homework.

'Oh, get away,' I muttered. 'Just go. Like now. Sometimes I can't stand the sight of you. And you've got that funny fungus smell again. You need aroma-therapy. Freshen you up. Let me get on with my work, George.'

But George, I knew he was called George, though I didn't know how I knew he was called George – didn't go away. He just stood there looking beseeching like

Please Help Me, Petra. Give me, gimme Something. But I didn't want to give him anything because I hadn't a clue what he wanted.

I put down my Biro. Henry VIII's wives would have to wait. (And why the hell were half of 'em called Catherine? Hadn't they any imagination in those days? What about Britney? Queen Britney? Beheaded? Not a good idea.) But I couldn't carry on with HOMEWORK. No one, not Shakespeare or even our headteacher, could cope with George staring at them.

'George,' I said gently. 'The answer's no. Like whatever it is you want I don't know it and I don't have it and I don't have the time. Clear? I don't want to solve your problems. You keep them. I've got my own. Like Henry VIII and maths.' Actually, I get Barney, my brother, to do maths for me, so that one's solved. But there's the rest. 'If it's the fight of good against evil don't ask me, I'm not noble enough, and sometimes I don't know which is which, specially when Seth's around and talking me into things. You can have all the magic spells. I don't want 'em. They're complicated. They only cause trouble. You 'ave 'em. Or Barney. I won't be like jealous. They're all yours. I don't do problem solving, George. I've got too much homework.'

George's eyes filled with watery sorrow. A pale, sick-looking aura flicked round his head and he flickered and wobbled. He seemed to be saying no, shaking his silly head and twisting his horrible cap round like crazy, trying to tell me something. I felt mean and wormy and a bit sick.

'I don't want to see you again! Ever! Never is too soon for me, George. Good-bye.'

But he didn't go. He just stood there, twisting his cap, goggle, goggle.

There's different ways of seeing. The OK kind. People: Granny reading a book, my kind teacher who died, Uncle Batty digging in the garden, the old corner sweet shop. Friends. I got friends. Hunter, my first little terrier, silly old George.

But there's the other seeings. Disasters, earthquakes, floods, volcanoes, hurricanes – I see them just before they come on telly, like 9/11 in America and the giant tsunami in the Indian Ocean. Thousands die. All I can do is cry.

Last week I woke up in the middle of the night and knew Grandpa had won something. I hoped it was the lottery, but it turned out to be a bottle of whisky. He was very pleased with it all the same, but then *he* hadn't thought of there being anything more than a bottle of whisky whereas I had. Then there's a beautiful lady I see in the park sometimes. She wears blue and a rainbow halo and smiles at me, as real as the other people walking around but she isn't, I know. I like seeing her. She makes me feel safe. But she doesn't come as often as she used to. I expect I'm getting too old. It might all go away soon.

I suppose it's a gift. But I didn't ask for it, did I? Any more than you ask for brown eyes instead of blue. I often wish it would go away. I don't want to be different. Who the hell wants to be different? Kids are often horrible to the ones who are different like Barney, but he doesn't notice, too busy thinking up the secrets of the universe, whereas I do notice. So I don't talk about it, my gift or whatever.

But I still see things even if I don't talk about them any more. They're part of my life. I can't help it if I'm different. I just have to get on with it. It doesn't scare me.

Long ago I talked to my Dad about seeing things. He listened to me very carefully. But what do I have to do? I asked him, for I was beginning then to realise how strange it was. I don't think you have to do anything, just accept them when they come, don't worry and don't be afraid. I told him that I wasn't, and that I didn't get scared. That's great, he said; and I'll say a prayer for you, Petra – for Pete's sake, he grinned. That's an old name joke. He helped me see that I wasn't a freak, or mad, but still Petra, his daughter and OK.

But I didn't tell him all of it . . . It might worry him

and it doesn't often happen. You see, and it's hard to explain – it's different and whereas the other things are *here* on this planet, this one is not. It's *not* here at all. I call it 'The Nothing'. And I'd told Dad that seeing things *doesn't* scare me. I could like manage them. But 'The Nothing' is different, it's out in space, in another dimension and it scares me rotten. I don't want to tell anyone about it, not even Dad, for I hope it will go away. For ever.

But as George stood twisting his cap round and round, there's a black flash in the corner of my left eye. I shut my eyes tight, trying not to notice. If I open them slowly it will go away taking George with it.

It's still there. But I won't take any notice of it. No. I refuse. I've got homework to do. And then another black flash in the corner of my left eye. I can't escape. I knew, somehow, that it was coming . . .

Out of the mist, seeping in, like water filling up a hollow slowly comes a picture, pale, like in old photos – a narrow, twisty, lonely lane winding uphill. It's muddy and desolate. Bare trees rise above high banks, branches black for Winter. Then out of the swirly mist a shadow girl comes running up the hill, a little dog on a lead scampering after her, trying to keep up on stumpy legs. I can't see her face, only her long dark hair streaming down her back. But even as she fades out of sight I hear the sound of an approaching car . . .

Another sound – louder – music playing. Seth's playing a heavy metal CD at full volume. He and Barney crash into the room. George disappears. I never see him go.

Chapter Two

How the hell could I cope with Seth standing there where George had stood a moment before, Seth grinning at me, Seth talking, talking as he always does? Seth's too much, always too much. I could see his mouth opening and closing, rubbish coming out. And there was still tons of homework to do.

'Get lost, Seth. Unless, unless, can you tell me the names of old Henry VIII's wives in the right order?'

'You must be joking, Pet. Who was Henry VIII anyway? Some old geezer?'

'I can tell you,' said Barney and he was off. 'Catherine of Aragon, Anne Boleyn, Jane Seymour, divorced, beheaded, died, Anne of Cleves, Catherine Howard, Katherine Parr, divorced, beheaded, died,' chanted Barney. He knew. He's a walking encyclopaedia. Why had I bothered to ask Seth? Oh, just to

12

stop him talking at me and calling me Pet.

'Come on. Leave the rubbish stuff, Pet, and let's go have a game,' cried Seth.

'You two can. I gotter finish this. And don't call me Pet!' I shouted.

'You work too hard. I don't believe in work,' Seth replied.

He doesn't believe in anything except Seth. He's rich, fit, gorgeous – all the girls go for him – and he's a total . . . (that word Mum won't let me use). Like George he's always around. Ever since he landed in my class. Who didn't like him – at least the boys didn't. He's been everywhere and boasts about it – Hollywood, New York, gambled at Las Vegas, Paris, Moscow, Rome . . . Seth had done everything, sung the songs, worn the T-shirt. He has loadsa pocket money and his mother, who came from South America and had been a beauty queen, said Seth, wore designer gear and didn't look like the other Mums.

'I've got an idea,' he said now.

'Treasure it, then. Take care of it. It might survive.'

'Shut up. Listen, Pet . . .'

'I'm listening . . . But don't call me Pet.'

'Why don't we use this gift of yours?'

'What gift? No one's given me a prezzie lately.'

'I don't mean that. I mean you seeing things . . .'

'I thought you didn't believe that I could.'

'Well – I've changed me mind. It was the other day when you knew about that tsunami in Asia before it came on the news . . .'

'Oh, shut up, willya? I don't talk about things like that any more.'

'Well, you should. To me, anyway. You see, at the moment it's not very useful, is it?'

'What d'you mean? Useful?'

'Your gift. I mean, you can't *do* anything about Africa or Asia, can you, Pet?'

'I can try, can't I? And I'm not your Pet. Or anyone else's. And shut up.'

But he carried on.

'Well, you could train it to *be* useful. Foretell things. Exam questions, the lottery draws, football results, horse racing details, everyday happenings. It would be fantastic, wouldn't it? We could be rich, successful and powerful. Totally cool!'

'I think you're disgusting, Seth!'

'No – listen – it makes sense.'

'No, it doesn't. First of all, I can't see things to order. Second, I've no control over it. Third, it would be wicked. Fourth, your family's loaded already, Seth.'

'Ah, but you and Barney could be rich, too. Since your dad's a vicar, you're all as poor as third world victims!'

'Did you mention me?' put in Barney. 'I don't care about being rich. It's not interesting like maths.'

'Oh, go back to your maths puzzles, Barney. It's only Seth being – like – evil as usual.'

'Oh, that,' said Barney.

'I think it could be brilliant . . .' Seth grinned.

'And I think it's wicked. You think I'm one.'

'That's because your dad's a vicar. You have to try to be good. It limits your thinking. I'm sorry for you, Pet.'

'Don't be. My dad's great, fantastic. I love him. And go home, it's time for you to go to your beddy-byes, Sethy-Wethy.'

'OK, OK, I'm off. But think about it, Pet . . .'

'DON'T CALL ME PET!'

'I'll talk to you again when you're in a better mood. And you look terrible. Greenish. You know I'm right. I always am.'

'See you!'

He's got a multi-coloured aura like Joseph's Technicolor Dreamcoat. But Barney doesn't have one. Sometimes I wonder if I made him up. But he seems real. Like a funny furry animal. Whereas Seth's like a film star leaping around, showing off, fighting duels and carrying off women. I once saw him suddenly clear as anything, swords flashing, etc. He was in the past and called Ronaldo, like a footballer. I did tell him about that one. At first he was dead pleased, then I said, 'He dropped his sword, ran away and hid. Up a tree.' He didn't like that. Stormed off in a mood, muttering rubbish, crap. Which is what he did now – good.

Chapter Three

Mad Jeffers kept us in for half an hour practising for the carol service. He was in a rotten mood and I had to sing my one solo verse four times before he said it would do, he supposed, sigh. Barney's lucky. No one gives him a solo. Voice like a smoke alarm. But he's on the drums in the orchestra. Seth's solo was OK, naturally, though they glared at each other and Seth kept pulling hideous faces every time Mad Jeffers turned his back for half a minute, for he'd had to take off his bone necklace and his rings including his earring at the beginning of the rehearsal. And hand over the ebony Egyptian cat he swears brings him luck. Mad J. is young and gym-fit – works out every day – dead keen, razor-edged monster, mad about fitness and even madder about music. Half a note out gives him spasms of agony. Music matters. Not kids.

Kids don't. Their only use is to make sounds. GOOD ONES. Today he lined us up and told us how useless, how crapulous, how totally, utterly feeble we were and (lifting his hands high and holding his little rhythm stick up to Heaven) he asked how we could have the unbelievable cheek to stand there and open our unlovely mouths in what passed for singing; it was beyond him, beyond anyone with an ear at all.

Mad Jeffers isn't like the other teachers. Maybe it's because he teaches music. 'I don't stand any nonsense,' he announces to every new class, waving his little rhythm stick at them. Although he's young, he's like an olde-worlde teacher. Wonder he doesn't wear a cap and gown all the time, like teachers in Victorian times with mortar boards.

'Only one of you has any talent whatsoever. Only one of you can act-u-all-y sing,' he hissed. 'And that boy – if *it* can be called a boy – blessed with this God-given gift is the worst-disciplined, idle, ignorant, disobedient creature it has ever been my misfortune to teach. You, Seth de Freitas, are a monster.'

'Yes, Sir,' smiled Seth, showing his perfect teeth. He doesn't need a brace, unlike half the class. 'You're right, Sir. Now can we go home, please? We've gone an hour over time already.'

'How dare you? How dare you question time?'

'I wouldn't do that, Sir. Very difficult thing to question is time, Sir,' murmured Seth, but Mad Jeffers wasn't listening, fortunately. Too busy talking.

'Just be grateful that you have the benefit of my tuition for those extra few minutes.'

He turned to the rest of us, who were not daring to fidget, but longing to go.

'Have you all forgotten, have you, that in a fort-night's time you will be performing in the cathedral in front of the Most Important People in the town?'

'Oh, them!' sighed Seth. 'Anybody interesting? Celebrities? Anyone who'll tape us for telly, then? Spot our fantastic talent?'

Mad Jeffers raised his eyes and his little stick to Heaven once more.

'Go. Go. Go. All of you. Before I go mad. What are you laughing at, boy? No, don't tell me. Just be here at the same time tomorrow.'

Seth went up to Mad J and held out his hand.

'My necklace, please, Sir. And my rings. And the cat.'

'I'd like to burn them. Wretched jewellery and trin-kets!'

'Not a good idea. I could sue.'

Mad Jeffers glared but handed over the necklace and the rings and the little black cat. We all shot out of the hall, only to be called back to walk steadily and silently, until at last we were outside in the pouring rain slashing down into the December dark and belting towards Mum holding open the door of the oldest and rustiest car in the world, of which Mum is possibly the worst driver in the world.

'Get in quick. It's a filthy night and we've got to hurry. And you're late. Get in, Seth. I'll drop you off.'

'Mad Jeffers kept us. The pig! You know what he's like.'

'He'll be worse before the end of term. There's so much going on. And he'll want everything PERFECT. Everyone gets nervous. Specially him.'

I got in the front, Seth and Barney in the back.

Mum swung out into the road, just missing the gatepost. Like I said, she is possibly the worst driver in the world. She teaches, but not in our school – whew – that would be *too* embarrassing.

The windscreen wipers whooshed steadily.

Mum was going a different way home today as the town was congested, it always is, but with Christmas near and the pouring rain it would be worse than usual. The road she took was narrow and twisty, just a back lane really. We didn't know it at all. And it was pitch black already. 'Which way?' she asked at a fork in the road. 'Left,' said Seth so she went left. I wasn't sure. There was something I knew about it, but I couldn't remember what. I looked back at Seth who was staring out of the car window. Barney was lost in his own geeky world as usual. Mum was leaning forward, concentrating hard, going fast through the rain down the narrow, uphill road. 'Slow down,' I said, but she didn't hear. I wanted her to cool it as we drove along because I knew there was something *UP*. Bad vibes all around, red alert signals switching on in my brain. A flash of lightning lit up the car. Lightning? In December? Mad, crazy. I could see the black streaks in Mum's aura. They'd been there when we got in the car but they were thicker, stronger now. The rain grew heavier, noisy on the car roof, slashing and stabbing, cold winter rain. She was going much too fast for this awful road. A pain like a knife stabbed in my chest.

'You sure we're going the right way, Mum?'

'Yes,' she snapped.

'Well, what's the hurry?' I muttered.

'We've got to go out. Remember? It's Grandad's birthday and we're treating him to a meal at Seth's dad's pub. But I didn't know the weather would be like this.'

'Are you sure we're on the right road?'

She didn't answer. I think we took the wrong turning.

The windscreen wipers whooshed madly. Rain lashed the windows. The air in the car thickened, smelling hot and sticky. Surely even those morons

Seth and Barney must notice! Lightning flashed and the streaks in Mum's aura slithered like Medusa's snaky locks – who the hell was Medusa? I only knew she'd got a bad hair problem. Like Mum at the moment. I was breathing hard, the pain in my chest worse now. Suddenly it was cold. Something was out there, I knew. Something bad. And whatever the thing out there was, it was almost on us . . .

'Pull in! Pull in, Mum! NOW!'

Blazing headlights tore the dark apart. Something loomed out of the black night. And behind the lights a monster, a dinosaur beast, a giant earth mover looming all over the road, overwhelming us, crushing anything in its way. Us!

Mum pulled in to the tall, sheltering wet bank, clutching the steering wheel as a huge juggernaut crawled past, taking over all the road. Only the tiny crossing place in the bank was saving us, tucked into the grass and mud, sheltered by the hedge and trees. We were OK, but only just, as the machine beast ground its way past, towering over our old rusty car. And it was gone. Seth swore and put a finger up to the machine now disappearing into the darkness. And we were OK. Safe.

'Nobody's driving it,' Barney squeaked.

'Course they are,' quivered Mum. 'There has to be.' She was slumped over the wheel, shaking. 'They should have dipped the lights. There's got to have been somebody in it.'

She started up the car.

'I think we took the wrong turn,' she admitted at last. Then:

'Is it all clear?' she asked me.

I peered through the windscreen to see if anything else was bearing down on us in the murky gloom. And it seems that a pale shadow hurries up the lane ahead of us, dark hair streaming, little dog scampering after her on stumpy legs. I hear a car approaching, the sound growing louder. The girl pauses, pulling the little dog into the bank, and then they fade away.

'No . . . no!' I cry.

But I make no sound. No one hears me.

It took a few revs to get the car out of the soft muddy ground but at last we were away.

'I'll have to reverse. And I hate it. I'm bad at it,' moaned Mum.

'I'll tell you what to do,' announced Seth.

My chest stopped hurting as Mum drove slowly and carefully home. I wasn't scared now. But I knew the thing hadn't got it in for *us*. I knew. It was all about me. What? And why?

Chapter Four

The Old Inn which belongs to Seth's stepdad is older than older than old. In the summer tourists arrive from all over the world saying 'Wow!' in American, French, Japanese, German, Icelandic, whatever, for it's got beams, huge fireplaces, twisty chimneys, an old granite cross and yes, you've guessed it – a ghost. Over the gynormous fireplace where you could burn whole forest trees is a date 1568, but that's recent, says Seth's stepdad, grinning, the Old Inn goes back much further than that, he tells the tourists who are wallowing in all the history and atmosphere.

'Used to hold human sacrifices. Beautiful girls sacrificed every spring to make the crops grow. Fertility rites. They say a witch was burned in there once . . .'

Then he laughs and tells them he's having them on

and the visitors relax a bit before he comes in with the clincher,

'But there IS a ghost.'

Intake of breath, oooooh!

'Really?'

'Really. It's a monk and it walks round the house and disappears into a door round the side then down into the cellar. The monks brewed beer and wine there. It's a boozy ghost!' He's beaming.

'Have you ever seen it?'

'No, but my son has – he'll tell you all about it. Here, Seth . . .'

And Seth does tell them all about it. He's got the spiel off by heart. I helped him make it up. Barney added dates and things.

Seth's stepdad, Mr de Freitas, bought the Old Inn and had it done up – it was almost derelict. He'd travelled all over the place, made tons of money and wanted to settle down. He spent thousands and then more thousands on advertising, Dad said. And Seth came to my school and landed up in my class, worse luck.

The first time I went to the new Old Inn I said, 'Oh, God. Wow!'

'I knew it would amaze you,' purred Seth. 'Fantastic, isn't it?'

But it wasn't the place being wonderful and fantastic

that made me say, 'Oh, God, wow.' It was the fact that I realised I'd been there before in the past and knew every inch of it. I'd no idea why, how and when . . . But I knew it well.

Seth showed us the huge ancient attics and I felt the fear of the Catholic priest hiding in the cupboard they called the priest hole and wild excitement at the tiny window where a landlady had climbed out to join her lover hiding below in the bushes!

I didn't let on except to Barney later and he said he'd read about the feeling and it was called déjà vu. Already seen.

Seth really hasn't got a clue. He reads fantasy books all the time, he writes fantasy stories at school, he collects charms and lucky objects from all over the world just like a magician and watches fantasy videos. But he doesn't know what I know, doesn't see what I see, doesn't feel what I feel.

'I shall make fantasy and horror films when I grow up. Probably win an Oscar,' he says, only half laughing.

He told everyone he was psychic. But I knew that he was about as psychic as a dung beetle.

Yet I like him. He makes me laugh. And with him around showing off no one takes too much notice of me. Or Barney. You see, I'm scared people will think me and Barney are weird, strange. Not that Barney cares anyway. But I do. And though sometimes Seth makes me mad I don't *really* mind. Underneath the boasting he's a bit lost at times, and scared of his step-father. Then he needs me and Barney. Mr de Freitas has power. He's big with a big personality. He enters a room and it's crowded. I think he could be a cruel man.

In summer the Old Inn is full of tourists, visitors, foreigners – it's near the sea here and people visit it a lot. In the winter it's almost empty, the fire blazes in the hearth, throwing flickering shadows into the dark corners. And there are shapes and sounds you can't really catch, they're always just fading away, disappearing round the corner, floating away into the furthest end of the ceiling. Out of the corner of your eye you see them, then when you really look, they've vanished into nothingness, leaving only the shape of something that was there before. Wraiths, they call them, the ghosts of ghosts. All those people . . . all those people . . . who lived there in the Old Inn.

Tonight was Grandad's seventieth birthday. His friend Arthur had come and some other old mates. The other uncles, Dad's brothers Joe and John, live too far away – but Aunt Cilla, Dad's sister, was there and Uncle Barry (Boring Baz), her partner. And Grandma, of course, a big lady. Dad hadn't got here yet – someone, somewhere was very ill, so Dad would be with them instead.

Grandad said he was going to have steak, egg and chips plus sausages and beans followed by blackberry and apple crumble, beer, whisky and coffee. He sat opening his prezzies, king of his space by the fire.

'Do you think that's a good idea?' asked Mum. 'It's not the right food for a man of your age.'

'I've been eating the wrong food all my life,' he chortled. 'So I'm not going to stop on my birthday, ho, ho, ho. You always were a misery, Annette. I'm going to have a great time. You see.'

There we sat, about a dozen of us round a big table underneath the window at the far side of the huge room, warmed by a great blazing fire in the old grate. Candles flickered as the wind zoomed round the old building that had sheltered people through the centuries. I bet someone like Grandad was there in the Middle Ages and before then, I thought. I bet he even lived in a cave and dragged off Grandma by her hair. Looking at her now sitting beside him, huge and stately like a cathedral and imagining this I spluttered a bit, choking on my food. Seth banged my back. Too hard. I shoved him off.

A sharp gust of wind bashed into the window with its little lead squares.

'This place is definitely haunted tonight,' said my

silly Aunt Cilla, who was wearing a nearly topless red dress that cheered up all the old boys. And Seth, who kept trying to peer down it.

'No such things as ghosts,' said boring Uncle Baz. I get angry if people say that vicars are boring. Boozy Uncle Baz is boring. So are the rest of them standing by the bar talking to Seth's stepdad. My dad looks after the junkies, the down-and-outs and the dying. They just drink and talk.

'We had a strange experience coming home along the lane,' began my mother. 'A monster machine thing – we didn't know it was coming what with the dark and the wind and the rain. If we hadn't pulled in . . .'

'I told her,' joined in Seth. 'I *knew* it was on its way. I knew it was dangerous. A monster ghost machine out to get us . . .'

He was standing up now, waving his arms, acting the monster machine, his eyes flashing, pushing back his long hair, glowing with it all – everyone listening, he'd got his audience. 'It was lucky I was there to tell . . .' Here he smiled at my mother, '. . . you to pull in. And you did. And here we are!'

I opened my mouth and closed it again. What was the use? If Seth said that was how it was – well, that's how everyone would think it was. And did I really care? Seth's a show-off, I know that. So? The wind whistled away in the background.

'It all happened so suddenly,' said Mum. 'I still don't know what I was doing, coming along that narrow back lane . . .' Her aura had gone very streaky.

Everyone was talking now at the top of their voices. I kept on eating.

'I'm psychic, you see,' Seth was saying to my sister Kate, who's older than me. 'I do see things. But I don't mind. It's interesting and it takes a lot to scare me.'

He smiled the beautiful smile which almost makes up for his conversation and she smiled back.

'I think I'm going to throw up,' I muttered to Barney.

'Take no notice of him. The food's great.'

Someone went out and a blast of cold air blew in. The windows rattled. I yawned. I was knackered, finished, and I'd got loads of homework waiting for me back home. Happy Birthday, Grandad, I thought, and please can I go now before the grown-ups get sloshed and Uncle Baz goes doolally as usual?

Then Barney asked if we could go on the fruit machine and I perked up for the moment. We got some change off everyone and headed for it, only to lose the lot in a matter of minutes.

'Well, that was fun while it lasted, I s'pose,' I sighed.

Seth appeared at my shoulder having stopped chatting up my sister.

'Lost, have we?' he said cheerfully. 'Let me show you how it's done.'

Naturally, after a few goes all the Triple Bars came in. The jackpot. Coins gushed out of the machine.

'You jammy git,' grumbled Barney.

'There's nothing jammy about it. It's skill, that's what it is, my friends.'

He pocketed his winnings and walked off, grinning. We looked at each other.

'Those who have it all . . .' I started.

'Those who don't have sod all . . .' he finished. For a vicar's son his language is awful.

We went over and sat down on the seats by the window. I stared through the little squares of the window with its deep stone sill. Suddenly the wind dropped, the rain stopped and it fell silent outside. It was very still out there. The chatter in the room faded away and it seemed to be growing lighter as the clouds cleared and the moon and stars began to appear. I knew what was coming. I'd seen it all before; these were old friends, not a black flash.

One monk led the way for the other six walking behind him two by two. He held a lantern hanging from a curved staff. Another monk swung a pot on a chain. Smoke spiralled out of the holes and I could smell sweetness. The two monks at the back carried a chest, black, with metal bands round it. They all wore black robes and the hoods covered their faces. They were blackness in darkness.

Chanting began. And I knew that chant although it was in Latin. I knew it because I'd heard it before, and because I'd always known it. Since for ever.

'Pray for us now and in the hour of our death,' sang in my head. They halted and one of those at the back lifted up his head and threw back his hood revealing that bald spot they all have in the middle. He peered at the window where I sat looking out into the night. I couldn't break away from his gaze. He knew all about me. Gregorius, he's called. Another friend.

I wasn't scared. The monks never scared me. Any more than George does. They're just there, part of the scenery. Cosy, really. My monk Gregorius wanted to tell me something – but the distance was too great between us. Yet I felt closer to him than the chatterers in the room behind me. Like George, my special monk was trying to ask me something. But I didn't know what. One of the other monks stumbled. The swinging pot sent up smoke, sparks and a flare of light. And in that thrown-up light I thought I saw a transparent George almost hidden by the folds of the monk's robe, funny sad George – a shadow of a ghost, or a ghost of a shadow? Was there – faintly – the fleeting shadow of a girl with long dark hair running up a lane followed by a little dog? Then the monks vanished. Noise returned.

'You were miles away.' Mum's hand was on my shoulder. Worrying, as usual.

'Petra's seeing things. Psychic, like me,' said Seth.

'You're not psychic, just sick,' grinned Barney.

'Leave him alone,' said Kate. I think she fancies Seth. 'I like his hair and his necklace.'

'Stick to your own boyfriends. You've got at least five,' I told her.

She giggled. We all giggled. Someone called out that it was time to go.

But the door flew open. A vision flew in. Smiles, hair, shape, eyes, she's got the lot. Always had had. Better than any TV presenter.

'Bella!' cried Grandad. 'I thought you weren't coming!'

'Of course I was coming. I wouldn't miss your birthday, you know that. Happy Birthday, Dad.'

She threw her arms round him and kissed him. His face shone.

Aunt Bella, my Dad's youngest sister, Grandad's favourite. She works on local radio. Behind, following her through the door came a pile of brilliantly wrapped presents. And behind them, ducking his head for he was much too tall for the ancient door-way, came a guy, smiling at us all, gorgeous enough even to be a match for Bella. Black. The handsomest man I've ever seen.

'Meet Gareth,' she cried. 'He's the man I'm going to marry!'

'Oh, no! You're the girl I'M going to marry!' he zipped back.

Shouting and laughing, more drinks all round, kissings. Mr de Freitas treated everyone in the pub to drinks for this special occasion. We wouldn't go home for ages now. Seth was scowling. He likes to be the star. But I shrank back into the heavy curtain drawn back against the window. I didn't want to look at this guy. Didn't want to join in. His aura. It was different, scary. I didn't want to know about it or him.

I'm knackered, I want to go home, I screamed inside. Let me out of here!

At that moment Mum's mobile rang. After a minute:

'That'll be Tom,' she sighed. 'Telling me he won't be able to make it. He never gets to anything. Sorry,' she said to Grandad, and then her face changed, she stopped smiling. Everyone shut up, trying to listen, wondering what Dad was saying. Then she closed up her mobile and faced us all. She looked shattered.

'A girl's missing,' she said. 'They're afraid she may have been abducted. But . . . but the last place she was seen was along that lane. The one where the horrible machine nearly ran us down.'

Silence. Then Seth spoke:

'I know. She was abducted by the monster machine with nobody driving it.'

'Oh, don't be so stupid, boy,' snapped his stepfather. Seth looked hurt.

Then noise exploded as everyone else spoke at once. In the middle of it all I could hear Grandad's deep voice.

'That's where that girl was murdered. About five, six years ago. Lovely girl. Looked like Kate.'

'Who looked like Kate?' asked Seth.

'This girl. She had long black hair. And she had a little dog. She was taking it for a walk. They never found her, only the dog.'

In the buzz that followed, I waited for the black flash. I knew it was coming. In my left eye first, as usual, then in my right eye. I knew it would come soon. It did.

A lane. Winter. But clearer with a little colour. A girl, long black hair hiding her face, runs up the hill in the lonely lane, the branches of the trees arching overhead. A little dog hurries after her. His lead is red. There's the sound of a car coming nearer, and she pulls the dog into the side of the bank for the lane is narrow. Her hair falls over her face so I can't see it clearly.

My eyes close. Then I open them . . . to find I'm looking straight into the remarkable eyes of Bella's man, Gareth.

I know he knows. He knows I can see. Because he can as well. His aura flickers and flashes. I wonder if he can see mine? Of course he can. I don't want him to know about me so I turn to the window looking for my friends, Gregorius the monk and George the poor pauper. *They* are my friends, I know. And I need them. For this Gareth, who's he? What's he doing here? But there's no sign of the monks. No sign of George.

Talking, talking, everyone's talking. Who is this girl? What has happened to her?

Every day we hear tales of children, teenagers, abducted, missing, murdered . . . Everyone's telling everyone else what should be done about it. I can hear Seth as he flings his hair around telling Kate what it's all about. I feel numb. I can't say anything. Seth pushes an alcopop at me and then another, but, at last, Mum hustles me and Barney to the old heavy door, covered in studs.

'We're going home,' she said.

Chapter Five

Friday night and
Saturday morning

We got home after midnight. Dad was still out, the
house empty. I went up to my bedroom at the top of
the house, an attic room, all beams and spiders.
Through the window you can see for miles and as I
drew the curtains, I could see far, far away the Tower
among the trees at the highest point of the hill. Vroom-
vroom went my head. I should never have let Seth talk
me into those alcopops. I knelt on the bed, wobbling a
bit, looking through the window and not wanting to
bother to undress. But the moon was bright, shining
on the Tower, making it stand out sharp and clear.

It's not always there. You can't always see it. I told
my mother about it once. She said I was making things
up as usual, she couldn't see it at all. That's because
you're blind as a bat, I told her, but not out loud.

'If you didn't spend so much time making things

up you might get on better at school. Look at Kate and Barney.'

'I don't want to,' I snapped back. 'You look at them!'

Sometimes I can't see the Tower. It disappears for weeks at a time, then it comes back. It was definitely there tonight. At last I climbed into bed with thoughts of the missing girl spinning round and round in my brain as if it was on a computer circuit; a lane, a girl, long dark hair, a monster machine, a litte dog, a car approaching. Who was the girl? The girl like Kate with long dark hair? Running . . . then missing . . . George, what are you trying to say to me, George, let . . . me . . . go . . . to . . . sleep.

George and Gregorius stand outside the Tower as I walk slowly up the path leading to it. My boots are weighted down with concrete so I'm very slow. But it's important to get there as Seth is beckoning to me to join him. I know they've come up from the Old Inn on a path that once ran long ago from the inn to our house and up to the Tower. But George and Gregorius lift their hands in the air, George's dirty, Gregorius's very clean. I can see their palms clearly as they push against the air, and shake their heads. I've got to go back down. Disappointed, I turn to go and the ground drops down, down, down in front of me . . . it's a precipice . . . I fall, fall, fall, screaming . . .

I woke up on the landing, swaying at the top of the stairs. I stopped screaming in a sec. I know I'm OK – just sleep-walking again. I'm fine, not to worry – you know what to do, Petra, just go back to bed – you're OK. Don't worry. You're fine. Just don't wake up Mum. She can't handle it. Can't handle me.

And my Dad came up the stairs.

'You OK?' he asked. 'The nightmare again?'

'Yeah. Sleepy now.'

'Go back to bed. You'll catch cold. I'll tuck you in.'

He settled the covers over me. He was still wearing his anorak.

'You going out, Dad?'

'No, just coming in. It was a long night.'

I remembered it all and sat up.

'What's happened? Tell me.'

'Tomorrow. Go to sleep now. I'm shattered and so are you.'

'Dad?'

'Go to *sleep*. We'll talk tomorrow. Go to sleep, Petra, for Pete's sake.' He smiled at our name joke.

'Night, Dad.' I was already dropping off.

'Night. Sleep tight, don't let the fleas bite. And God bless.'

I woke late. Dad was eating breakfast when I got downstairs. Barney was up, a geek mole with sello-taped specs. Mum hovered round Dad like a child-minder. No Kate.

'Dad,' I began, grabbing the cornflakes.

'Don't bother your father!'

'It's OK. I want to talk to them anyway. Kate?' he said.

'I'll get her,' Mum hurried away.

Kate yawned and stretched into the kitchen. She looked terrible, blotchy and red-eyed.

'Dad, who is it? It's someone I know, isn't it?' she asked.

'You mustn't be upset. She's probably all right and will be back home in no time.'

'What's she called?'

'Laura Page.'

'Oh, no. She's in my class. I talked to her yesterday. She'll be OK, won't she? Won't she?'

'She's probably just run away. What's she like?'

'Nice. Got a boyfriend called James Munro. Dad, I bet they ran away together – she's a bit crazy.'

'They've checked with James Munro. He's still at home so she hasn't run off with him. Do you know anything else about her?'

'Not really. She doesn't go around with my lot. She's a Goth.'

'I knew it,' cried Mum. 'I don't like this gang stuff. What are Goths?'

'The opposite of Townies. Mum, I don't want to talk about it.'

'Kate, we do need to know about her,' Dad smiled at her. 'And you?'

'Kate's going out with a Goth,' Barney muttered, out of the blue. I was gobsmacked. What had got into him? We'd promised Kate we wouldn't tell anyone. 'It's, it's d-d-different now, Petra. Don't look at me like that.'

'Only a couple of times,' Kate shouted.

'Don't cry. Eat your breakfast.'

'I don't want anything. I can't eat anything!' Kate rushed out of the room, Mum running after her.

'Now tell me what you know about the Goths and the Townies, Petra.'

'Well, you can't lump them together like that.'

'Try.'

'Well, Goths wear black. They wear jewellery . . .'

'Paint their faces white,' put in Barney. 'They're nutty.'

'He's got it all wrong. Goths are interesting, really. They're individuals. They think about the planet and want to stop people killing it . . .'

'Music. They like freaky music,' said Barney. 'I'll tell you all about it if you like . . .'

'That's all right. I'll take your word for the freaky

41

music, Barney. Then how are Townies different, Petra?'

'Oh – well . . .' I didn't know quite how to describe them. '. . . oh, they move in groups, in crowds, do everything together. They wear much neater clothes, make-up. Sometimes they're sporty. Sometimes they're posh, but they can be dead common, Dad. Oh, it's difficult to explain. You know the difference when you see them.'

Mum came in with Kate in tow, pale but dressed and calm.

'Try to eat some breakfast,' Mum said. 'Please. And don't worry. It'll be fine. You'll see.'

Kate looked at her as if she was mad, but she drank her orange juice and nibbled at the toast. Dad stood up to go again.

'Thanks. I get the idea. Listen. Now Laura may just have run away but we can't take any chances. Don't mess about in town. Don't hang round street corners. It gets dark early, so get back early if you go out. And if you do know or find out anything let us know, won't you? Barney, are you falling asleep?'

Barney had got his eyes-half-closed, mouth-half-open look that gives people, Seth says, the idea that he's intellectually challenged or a halfwit.

'I've told them all that before,' Mum said. 'They do know. They're not little kids.'

'Neither was Laura Page.'

Dad looked at his watch, kissed Mum on her left ear and said:

'Don't know when I'll be back. Take care.'

And he was gone. Kate stuck up a finger after him.

'Don't do that,' Mum snapped. 'Your Dad's right. Just take care.'

Chapter Six

I wished for the twentieth time that morning that I
hadn't let Seth talk me into the alcopops the night
before. I felt dazed and dopey and promised never,
never again would I listen to him. Seeing George after
breakfast hadn't helped, either. He looked like I felt.
Sort of mouldering. I was trying to watch the news
about the missing girl and his greenish face kept getting in the way. There must be easier ways of living, I
moaned at him, and he disappeared as Mum entered
the room. Then Seth rang up to remind me that Mad
Jeffers was making us rehearse the cathedral carol
service this morning – such cheek on a Saturday. He,
Seth, thought we ought to be paid for it, and he
wished I'd get a mobile and then he could text me at
any time. I'd heard all this before and told him *again*
that Mum had said we couldn't afford one for me,

and Kate had only just had one for her last birthday
. . . So. Seth went on to say that he had lots of ideas
about the kidnap or the murder, whichever it was –
of course, she hadn't just run away, he, Seth, knew
this and we must gather all the info we could at
school and then make plans in the attic of the Old
Inn and had I got any ideas? No, only a headache, I
answered, told him I'd got to help Mum clear up and
I'll see him at rehearsal, and rang off when he asked
why we hadn't got cleaners to do the housework.

Mum dropped us off as she was going into school
anyway for a meeting. I wanted her to drive along *the*
road of the night before but she said she wanted to
do the ordinary, quicker way and that the lane was
probably full of police, etc.

We waited around outside, for the doors were still
locked. Everywhere looked grey, including our faces,
and a chilly wind blew round the corner bringing
spots of rain with it. I'd thought all the kids would be
milling around like they do at exam time, but no,
they were quiet and subdued and after a while I
realised they were afraid.

Seth was muttering angrily. Seth doesn't like to be
kept waiting, especially on a Saturday morning, oh
no. I told him there was nothing I could do about it
and would he shut up. Then Mad Jeffers appeared

with the caretaker, Mrs Blessed, the door was unlocked and we streamed inside and took our places.

'This will be disgusting,' Seth went on muttering, despite Mad Jeffers requesting silence. 'He's in an even worse mood than usual.' And he stuck his elbow into my ribs to make sure I got the message.

But the message I got wasn't from Seth. Instead, a black flash in the corner of my left eye. No, no, I don't want this. I'm not going to take any notice. But even as I shut my eyes to keep it out, another flash comes in the right eye and I'm cold, oh so cold . . .

A wild, black night, a wind blowing down a lonely lane and crawling down the hill comes an earthmover, huge as a dinosaur, the same monstrous devil machine in that tiny lane, towering as high as the banks with the trees overhead. The fear I felt before sweeps over me – I shall be crushed into nothing . . . I close my eyes to shut it far away and when I open them the wild night and the fearful machine have vanished and I'm looking at a narrow lane up which a girl with long dark hair is running, a little dog on a red lead scampering after her.

Oh, no, no, no, no, no, I'm not, I can't be, seeing the missing girl!

My head cleared. OK. OK. Seth was still digging me

in the ribs and singing at the top of his voice. I was in the hall. It was carol practice.

'Sing up,' sang Seth. 'Mad Jeffers is watching you. You looked horrible. White as a ghost and not blinking. Come on. Sing!'

Oh, little town of Bethlehem?

I managed to join in:

> How still we see thee lie,
> Beneath thy deep and dreamless sleep . . .
> The silent stars go by
> Yet in thy deep sleep . . .

'What the hell was up with you, Pet? Keep singing, nut face.'

> Yet in thy deep sleep shineth
> The everlasting light,
> The hopes and fears
> Of all the years,
> Are met in thee tonight.

That's just what I don't want, I cried inside, these hopes and fears things. Seth, help me. Then Seth started to sing his solo and I could let go, relax. Mad Jeffers was watching *him*. I was fine now. Nothing was wrong. Only I was very tired. I felt yellow, sick, wormy.

Mad Jeffers looked at me.

'I don't think you're up to singing your solo, are you?'

'No, Sir.'

'Then I'll give it to someone else, if you like.'

'Yes, please,' I muttered.

He sounded almost kind.

The carol rehearsal finished at last.

'Don't tell anyone I acted crazy,' I told Seth.

'No difference. You always do. What did you see, Pet? Tell me.'

I was so tired. Too tired to talk. I turned away from him and went up to Mad Jeffers.

'Sir, I'm going to be sick.'

'Nonsense.'

Then he looked at me.

'Yes. I see you are. Move out of the way, children. Let her through, now.'

I reached the toilets just in time.

Chapter Seven

*Saturday afternoon
and Sunday*

Once it got started the rain poured down steadily that Saturday, cold and mean, making me glad to stay in because I felt rotten and I didn't want to hear any more news of Laura Page, unless it was that she'd come home and was safe. Most of all I didn't want to see Seth and listen to his ideas on solving the mystery or using my 'gift' to get rich and successful or see the perfect teeth grinning in his dark face, like his mother's. So I snuggled down under the bedclothes with a hot-water bottle and Puddy-Cat keeping me warm. I peeped out once to see if the Tower was around but it was rain, rain, rain all the way so I didn't bother again. I'd got all my favourite books around me and my headphones handy for when I wanted to listen and I told Barney to tell Seth I was asleep if he called round. And that maybe I'd got some infectious illness. That would keep him away 'cos he's a terrible coward and is scared stiff of catching anything. So I slept a bit and read a bit and listened a bit. Perfect.

Even George didn't visit me.

Next day Dad said that I didn't have to go to the family service he takes on Sunday and Mum let me have a lie in.

But by Sunday afternoon the rain had stopped, the sun came out and shone its December shining and I felt bored and wanted to go out so I didn't really mind when Seth arrived. I put on my boots while he and Kate started to talk about what I supposed everybody was talking about, Laura missing, and then I noticed that he'd grown as tall now as Kate, possibly taller. He'd just about manage those solos in the cathedral carol service before his voice broke, I thought, and THEN I hoped he and Kate weren't going to begin carrying on – that would be too gross. It was the way they were looking at each other, but no go, as she's years older than him. Most of the boys his age were smaller than me, but not Seth, of course. As for me, I didn't like the growing stuff though being taller would be OK, but I didn't want balcony boobs like Kate and I hate nail varnish and lipstick, yuck. I'd rather have George than all that.

We set off for the park. Barney didn't want to

come. He wanted a go on the computer with no one else around.

'Don't be long,' called Mum. 'It'll soon be dark. And don't wander off. Promise!'

'Promise,' I called back to her.

'I promise if we catch a serial killer we'll bring him with us for tea,' grinned Seth, though he stopped grinning when I kicked his shin with my boot and he yelped instead – ouch!

'Don't say things like that to my mother. She doesn't know how to take them and gets bothered.'

'But you hurt me!'

'Tough.'

We ran down the road to Colin's, the newsagent, where Seth, who's always loaded, bought drinks, crisps, sweets, chocs for all of us – he's not mean even if he's wicked.

'Why aren't you obese?' I asked him.

'Wot? *Moi?* How can you think of such a thing?'

'Because the things you eat are the ones they're always banging on about.'

'Oh, shut up and enjoy yourself, Pet. You're such a misery. Must run in the family.' I went for him but he dashed over the road fast, grabbing Kate's hand, dragging her with him seconds ahead of a car driving too fast down the road. Petrified, I stayed safely on the other side while he gibbered up and down making monkey noises at me and scratching. Two white-haired old ladies walking past and glared at him.

'Youth today,' I heard one say. 'They're disgust-ing.'

'Yes, I agree,' yelled Seth. 'The older generation is shocking. Not like they used to be at all. I don't know what they're coming to.'

Once in the park we headed for the duck pond where Seth threw the ducks some broken-up custard creams.

'Stop it! They're bad for them. Custard creams!' cried Kate.

'I hate them, so the ducks are welcome. They like them all gooey in the water.'

We sat drinking on a bench while Kate told us about going out with Henry the Goth and how she thought of becoming one herself. I was glad she was talking so Seth wouldn't start on his ideas.

'Bad idea,' I said. 'Means trouble.'

'You'd do better with me than Henry,' said Seth, which gave Kate an attack of the giggles till she choked on a crisp. When she stopped coughing, with us banging her back, it was then I realised how quiet the park was except for us and the row we were mak-ing. The winding paths were empty now. No one walked among the trees on the hill. I saw the Decem-ber evening was darkening and I remembered the missing girl and I was scared. What had Dad said? And what Grandad had said about another girl who was never found. I didn't want to get shut in the park when they locked the gates and be never found, no way. Time to head home.

'Let's go. It's getting dark. They'll be mad with us.'

Kate and I stood up but Seth stayed put and broke into pieces a big bar of chocolate and started to hand us some each.

'I don't really want any more, thanks, Seth.' My stomach was still wobbly and I didn't fancy anything. 'Come on.' I was getting fed up with hanging about.

'We'll have it then.' He handed lots of pieces over to Kate. I looked up at the hill again. Somehow I couldn't take my eyes off it and as I watched I saw someone slip from behind one tree to another. Dad's warning sounded in my head-take care, come home early.

'Come on, you two!'

'What's the rush?' Seth drawled in the middle of describing how he'd wanted to have a go on the barman's Harley Davidson. But I'd seen two more figures moving through the trees on the hill – flat, twiggy shapes I didn't care for at all. Light was leaving the park. Soon it would be dark except for the lights on the road and the cars going past.

'Come on! We'll be locked in!'

'Then we'll climb out.'

'Those railings are really high. Oh, *come* on!'

It seemed to me that more shapes were gathering up among the trees and starting to move down the hill towards us.

'I think they're after us.' My red alerts were sounding now. Trouble. Big Trouble.

'Stop fussing, Pet – we'll soon be out of the park. Nobody's following us. Nobody there! You're just seeing things again, aren't you? They're not real!'

'Oh, no? They look real to me! How real is reality, Seth?'

There were lots of figures now, coming towards us. And they scared me. They looked dangerous.

'Run,' Seth yelled. 'Run. Follow me!'

'Oh, help,' cried Kate. 'Townies!'

'Yeah, that's us,' came a voice right behind us. 'Hand over anything you've got. Goths deserve to be punished.'

'I'm not a Goth!' yelled Kate.

'But you've got a Goth boyfriend. That's as bad.'

The speaking one was big, very big, wearing a back-to-front baseball cap, combat jeans, huge Nikes. We're in real trouble here, I thought, as he went to grab Kate.

'Seth! Help! Seth!'

But Seth was way ahead, moving on his new long legs, increasing the distance between him and the gathering Townies. And us. Leaving us all behind, heading himself for the fence and safety.

But when there's trouble, I go mad and turn on what troubles me. I kicked at the big Townie's knees with my big boots and he stumbled, toppling over another one, both of them falling in a heap, Kate's chocolates showering over them.

'Run! Kate! Run!'

And we ran. Like cheetahs on speed, heading for the railings beside the pavement, lights and people and safety, the Townies chasing us. Fast, faster, still ahead, but starting to get a stitch. Could we make it? I glanced behind and saw lots of them, all bigger than us.

Panting, with stitch hurting, we pounded on, nearly there but no way could we leap over those close-together railings with spikes on top. Swerving, I pushed Kate to the right.

'The gate,' I spluttered. Kate shot on her way towards it. But would it still be open? If not, we were finished, done for.

There was a gap. The gate WAS open – but Big Townie was almost on us, reaching out for Kate, grabbing her shoulder. Oh, help, help, we're done for.

A car horn hooted. A sleek, silver car drew in

beside the gate and as we crashed through the gap its door opened, a long pair of legs shot out, belonging to the six foot two plus of Bella's bloke Gareth.

'Need a lift?' he grinned.

'Please, oh, please,' we panted.

As we piled into the car the Townie pack turned, ran, disappeared.

'Where to?' he asked. I looked for Seth, but he was nowhere to be seen.

'Anywhere. Just away from here,' we answered, and he drove away.

I sat in the back. I couldn't stop staring at him.

'You'll know me next time!' He'd caught my eye in the mirror.

'Y-y-yes,' I muttered.

'Just like I know you. Come back to my flat. Bella's there and she'd love to see you.'

Chapter Eight

We'd not been to Gareth's flat before and I was curious about it, wary, suspicious; would it be strange? I expected it to be different, weird, maybe sinister, black magicky or space-age, designed by Doctor Who in an adventure-free moment. But it was ordinary, comfortable, lots of books, CDs, a Playstation, flowers on the balcony, nothing mysterious or peculiar. Gareth knocked us up some super grub – not curried bubonic plague made from weapons of mass destruction.

Bella had got wedding gear stuff, catalogues and bits of material piled up all over a sofa big enough for eight people which she and Kate nose-dived into making snuffling noises, while I watched *EastEnders* on a Goliath sized TV set. I glued my eyes to it pretending it was one of my all-time top favourite programmes. This was so that I didn't have to look or talk to Gareth or look at wedding dresses. If Bella hadn't been there I'd've exited out of that place fast, but he wouldn't harm us with Bella around, he wouldn't dare (would he?). Question: why would he, anyway? He was teasing her saying he'd turn up to their wedding in torn-off jeans, a dirty T-shirt and bare feet.

'Well, *you* can if you like. But *I'm* wearing something like this.' She held up a photo of a mist cloud. 'And Kate is choosing hers *now*. Lemon, we think.'

Pink was right for Bella, I knew. Her aura colour. Not that I wanted to know. Sometimes I got sick of knowing things. Unfortunately, I did: palest pink and white for Bella, lemon for Kate. I tried to concentrate on *EastEnders* instead.

'What's Petra wearing to this do?'

'I don't know. I don't want to dress up.'

'Really? You're different, then?'

'Oh, yes, she's different all right,' said Kate, draping something over her head. 'She like sees . . . things differently,' she finished quickly.

'Shuddup,' I snarled.

'Hey,' Bella cried, 'I found a "Wow" dress in the catalogue! It's lovely, isn't it, Kate?'

'Divine!'

I didn't think I could take much more of this so I

asked to go to the bathroom. That was ordinary, too. I'd expected something like Fungus the Bogeyman. But it was the same as ours at home, only cleaner and newer. Ours is old and murky.

When I came out loud music was playing in the lounge – one of Bella's favourites. I hesitated for a moment. I didn't much want to go back to *EastEnders*, wedding dresses and ghastly music. The door next to the bathroom was partly open so – wanting to, but not wanting to – I peered inside. I didn't mean to but it was like a sort of doom. I couldn't *not* peer inside even if HE did come along and splatter me.

I was in Gareth's study – at least there was a desk, an easy chair, computer, CD player, a bookshelf full of books and tapes, a filing cabinet, a phone. It was very tidy. There was only a calendar, a tray of pens and pencils and a folder on the desk. I looked at the folder. Then I opened it. 'New Clues in the Case of Missing Schoolgirl,' it read, 'Case to be Re-opened', and inside, a collection of photographs and news-paper cuttings. A phone rang and I jumped a mile in the air. I couldn't bear HIM to fmd me there. I shot out of the room, my heart racing and banging. *What* was Gareth doing? *Who* was Gareth?

Back in the lounge Kate was talking on her mobile.

'That was Mum. I said we'd be back soon. So we'd better go.'

59

'Don't hurry,' Gareth said. 'You're always welcome here.'

My head hurt as we drove home. It's not keen on thinking and it was having to.

In the car I watched the back of his head, daring to look properly at last, but I couldn't see much because of the high seat-backs. I closed my eyes as jagged gold flashes shot before them. Home, please, I thought. I'm knackered, no more ideas. Let Seth 'ave 'em. I'll donate them to him.

But Gareth knew I'd been watching him.

'Have I passed the test, Petra?'

'What test?' I stammered. 'We've already done most of them this term.'

'But there are tests all the time, Petra,' he said as he and Bella dropped us off at home.

Later that night Mum came up.

'Mum,' I said as she reached the door. 'I don't want Aunt Bella to marry that man.'

'Why ever not? He seems very nice. She's lucky. He's handsome *and* rich – not that *that* matters, of course!'

'You and Dad are always going on about money!'

'That's different. That's because of *children* and what they cost.'

'Oh, yeah, I knew it would come down to that.'

'But I don't see what you've got against Gareth.'

'I don't trust him. His aura . . .'

'Don't you start that again! I don't want to hear about it. You and Seth and your daft ideas. Just concentrate on your work and doing well at school. Forget auras, ghosts and all that rubbish.'

She was just about to slam the door.

'But who is he, Mum?'

'Who are you? Some Victorian strict father? You're a bit out of date, aren't you? If your grandad doesn't mind him, and he *is* Bella's dad, it's his business. Not yours. And your dad likes him. So go to sleep, Petra. And no sleep-walking tonight!'

I cried a bit in bed. I know Mum doesn't love me as much as pretty Kate and barmy Barney. Then Dad poked his nose round the door.

'Night! Don't let the fleas bite.'

'Fleas aren't my problem, Dad.'

'I know,' he said. 'But it'll be all right. You're a rock, Petra, though you don't know it yet.'

I wasn't sure I wanted to be a rock, somehow.

'Dad, can we pray for Laura Page? Not to be dead, but to come home safely.'

'Yes, that's what we'll do.'

So we did. That night I slept peacefully – no nightmares, no sleep-walking, not even a dream. When I woke up I thought about Christmas coming soon and what prezzies I'd like (*not* what I'd probably get. Mum doesn't believe in material possessions and Dad never thinks of 'em). But Grandad and Gran – their prezzies are always a bit different.

Chapter Nine

Monday morning

School was full of talk about Laura Page. School was
on the national news, School was famous. I didn't
want to know. In class Mrs Matthews called me over
to her desk.

'I know Laura's disappearance is worrying for us
all. But is anything else the matter, Petra? You look
tired and this work isn't very good, is it?'

'No, Mrs Matthews,' I answered both her questions.

'Is there any trouble at home?'

'No, Mrs Matthews.'

'Can I help in any way if there is anything worrying you?'

'No, Mrs Matthews.'

'Please let me know if you've got problems?'

'Yes, Mrs Matthews.'

She gave up and I dragged back to my desk. I felt as if I was hauling a heavy weight round with me. The day dragged along like a snake with bellyache from swallowing too much, and like the snake, I'd bitten off more than I could chew, what with my family, school, the girl in the lane, monks, Christmas rehearsals, homework, etc, etc. I couldn't get to grips with it all. I'd wanted to mitch off school for a day and run on a beach by the sea, for ever and ever over golden sands, running, running till all the murk went away and at the end waiting for me would be Christmas Day, with everything sorted and dozens of presents.

Not likely. I was in the classroom with my D essay and Mrs M. saying:

'Come out, Seth. I'd like you to read one of your stories out loud to the class, show them how it's done!'

Yuck! I still hadn't spoken to him after the way he'd deserted Kate and me when the Townies came after us.

It was one of his fantasies: Seth the Good fighting evil with his necklace, his Egyptian cat, his golden cup, his spear, several rings and his own Incredible Courage and Daring, to be rewarded with Ethelfleda, an Anglo-Saxon princess who loved him above all.

The class applauded when he finished and he did

his bow, hair falling, eyes shining.

'I'm going to enter that wonderful story for the festival after Christmas,' Mrs Matthews chatted on. Unlike Mad Jeffers, she's a great fan of Seth. 'It should do well. Did you like it, Petra? Didn't you find it a wonderful story?'

'Yes, Mrs Matthews,' I answered.

'Good. I wish you'd contribute a bit more, Petra, to the class discussion. You ought to give out ideas more, consider possibilities, work out answers for and against what you believe in. Do you agree?'

'Yes, Mrs Matthews,' I said. As far as I could see the answer was always either 'Yes' or 'No' so I picked on 'Yes'. She's a nice lady, Mum says.

'Tell me, Petra. what did you think of Seth's story? Strong stuff, isn't it?'

'Yes, Mrs Matthews.'

'Don't you wish you'd got his imagination, Petra?'

At last, 'Yes, Mrs Matthews, I do. I do wish I'd got his imagination.'

Oh, yeah, oh, yeah, yeah – please. For I could do without this stuff 'imagination' she kept on about, and Seth has the imagination of a dung-beetle. And everything Seth digs up has been buried long ago by someone else ready for him to scavenge and tell everyone it's his. So let me swap mine for his. Please.

'Well, keep on trying. Read lots and look at the

wonderful world around you and how magical it can be and you may be able to write a poem or story nearly as good as Seth's.'

'Yes, Mrs Matthews,' I said.

By the end of the morning I detested Mrs Matthews and Seth with her. I decided to send them both to a slug collecting farm (if I could find one). But Seth waylaid me on the way to lunch.

'Get lost,' I said. 'Whatever it is you want to do or say I want the opposite. You are a pain, Seth de Freitas. And I hate school. And you!'

'Look, it's not my fault if Madame Matt thinks I'm a genius. But you're obviously in a bad mood. Let me make it up to you.'

'You couldn't. The only way you could make it up to me is by ceasing to exist. I'd rather have George.'

'That's cruel. Don't be so mean. Come on. I've got something to show you and I'm taking you out to lunch.'

'I can't just walk out of school dinner like that. You have to have permission.'

'I already have, little Pet. Hey, don't kick me.'

'Well, no "little Petting" then. It makes me vomit. And we can't just go out of school like that.'

'Yes, we can. I rang Mum on my mobile . . .'

' . . . you're not supposed to have it in school . . .'

' . . . I'm different. Rules aren't for *MOI*. And Mum

rang my radiant and lovely fan club Ma Matty, so
you and I have permission to go to my home for
lunch. And so, Old Inn, here we come. Oh, I've got a
lift laid on as well. Biggins, Mum's odd-job man, is
probably waiting for us now at the gate.'

'You utter . . .'

'You're not supposed to use that word, Petra dear.
Not suitable for vicars' daughters.'

The Old Inn Volvo was waiting at the gate. So was
Barney. He got in with us.

'Where are you off to?'

'Seth's Magical Mystery Tour!' I muttered.

'Oh, I'm coming as well. Nobody'll miss me. They
never know if I'm there or not. What's all this
about?'

'Seth showing off,' I replied.

'Barney, you're coming to lunch and I'm showing
you something. And shut up, PETRA STEVENS, you
don't deserve a friend like *MOI*.'

We drew up at the Old Inn.

'Now what?' I asked.

'There,' Seth said. 'Look over there. On the hill in
that field behind the pub. See?'

'It's some sort of farm vehicle,' Barney said. 'So?'

'Come and look at it. Come on!'

'Why? I'm not into tractors or whatever,' I
snapped.

'Just come and look.'

'I want something to eat. I'm starving,' grumbled Barney. 'You promised a lunch.'

'I'm not walking through that mud just to look at a tractor. I wish I'd stayed at school.'

'Just come. Then we'll eat.'

So we walked up the hill, keeping to the hedgerow, till finally, out of breath, we got to the top and reached the machine. Close up it was enormous, giant sized.

'See,' panted Seth. 'It's the monster machine from the lane that night. The one that abducted that girl!'

Chapter Ten

Monday lunchtime

Oh, yes. It was the monster machine all right. Every hair on the back of my neck twitched and tingled. My brain went on red alert – trouble, trouble. I waited for the girl with long dark hair to appear.

But she didn't. And as I looked at the machine the twitches and alerts died down, faded out, vamoosed. But Seth was jumping up and down with satisfaction, sending up a lot of mud. Seth was even more pleased with Seth than usual. I could tell he was waiting for me to say something. So I didn't.

'What is it?' Barney asked.

'Dunno. I'm not well up on vehicles – tractors, earth movers, combine harvesters – what does it matter? It's THE monster machine. Do you think we should check it for clues or ring the police?'

'They might do you for time wasting,' said Barney.

The Bill's his favourite programme.

'Anyway, just 'cos we saw it that night doesn't mean it's got anything to do with Laura Page. We've seen it, Seth, so let's go and get some lunch.' My stomach was rumbling by now. After the walk and the climb up the hill I was even hungrier than I'd been before. And still fed up. What was I doing there, muddy and looking at a horrible great machine?

Seth took no notice. He'd climbed up on to the monster machine and was examining under the seat and round the controls.

'Look, there's a cigarette packet here and a bit of hair. Might be evidence.'

'Well, bag it up, Sherlock Holmes,' said Barney.

We waited for about five minutes. Then I said:

'C'mon, Seth. We're going now.'

'OK. OK. I'm finished now, anyway.'

Seth jumped down clutching the few objects he'd collected and we rushed down the hill to the Old Inn.

It was busy in there that lunchtime. I felt awkward going inside wearing my school uniform, as if I shouldn't be there. Seth didn't suffer from any such problem, however, striding in confidently as if he owned the place, which he probably did, and heading straight up to the bar. The Harley Davidson barman saw him straight away and came over to serve him.

'Hello, Seth. What can I get you?'

Seth looked round at us.

'What do you fancy?'

'Can I have a lemonade?' I asked.

'Sure. And you, Barney?'

'I'll have a coke, thanks.'

'OK. I'll have a shandy. And can we have three of those baguettes as well? There, Pet. You won't be hungry after you've eaten one of those, I can guarantee.'

'Why aren't you in school?' a voice snapped in my ear. It belonged to a woman who'd got 'I hate children' written all over her. I jumped a mile back but Seth turned and addressed her in his poshest voice:

'I'll have you know, madam, that this is lunchtime and my father owns this establishment so I have every right to be here, thank you. It's home to me.'

We collected our food and drinks and went to sit down leaving the woman gobsmacked. I took a bite of my huge baguette, which was delicious, and looked round the pub. There was no sign of Seth's step-dad there today. He'd gone to a meeting, thank goodness, Seth said. Sad that he and his stepfather didn't get on, I thought, thinking of my great relationship with my dad. Mind you, his mum was very fond of him, smiling as she greeted us. Boring, boozy Uncle Baz was there of course, glass in hand. He saw us and waved.

'He's had a few already,' muttered Barney.

I felt happy sitting in there watching the people go by and eating my lunch. I liked being in the Old Inn. It was a long way away from school and Mrs Matthews. There was a spooky song playing on the jukebox – I didn't know what it was but I liked organ music with a haunting sound. I sat there lost in thought and as the song ended the familiar face of George started to appear. Not today, George, I thought. Not here. Leave me in peace to enjoy my food. Don't bother me now. But his face suddenly appeared clearly, cap on his head and jabbing in the direction of the door. I looked to see what he was pointing at and he disappeared.

Gareth had just entered the pub.

He walked up to the bar, but didn't order a drink, just stood there gazing round as if he was looking for somebody. He glanced in our direction, but I shrank back and he didn't really know Seth or Barney. It wasn't us he wanted.

'What's he doing here?' I whispered.

'What do you think? Why do people go to pubs?' grinned Seth. 'He seems to be looking for someone.'

'Who cares?' shrugged Barney. He and Seth then started to chat, but I didn't hear them. I just watched Gareth. For the red alerts were working overtime now. Trouble. Trouble. He seemed to be looking at this man wearing a parka, jeans and wellington boots. Why? I felt this was very strange. His aura sort of jolted. Something was going to happen. It did. A few minutes later the door of the Old Inn flew open and a group of policemen shot in, one holding on to an Alsatian. Everybody in the pub stopped what they were doing and looked round.

'What the hell?' asked Seth.

'It's a raid,' said Barney. 'It's just like in *The Bill*.'

Perhaps they were after Gareth, I thought. I wouldn't put anything past him. He was capable of murder? No, I didn't want to think that.

But they headed straight for the man Gareth had been looking at, grabbed him and frogmarched him outside. Everyone else just stayed where they were, motionless, not knowing what to do. It was as if time had stood still. I felt dazed and confused. What was happening? Then, slowly, everything started to move again. I looked round for Gareth, but he had gone. No sign of him.

'Oh, no. Look at the time. We'll be late,' said Barney, looking at his watch. We'd forgotten all about school.

'Yeah, better get moving,' said Seth. 'Biggins has gone now.' He waved goodbye to his mum and we shot out of the pub and sprinted back towards school.

'I just had a thought,' panted Seth as we entered the school gates.

'What?' I gasped, out of breath.

'That man they arrested. He might be the monster machine driver. If he was, it'll show my old man. Calling me stupid.'

'He might be anybody,' I said.

'Well, he was dressed like a tractor driver, wasn't he?'

'So that makes him a kidnapper, I s'pose,' I said.

We were late getting back and we got a rollicking from Mrs Matthews.

On the late news that night a report came in that a forty-year-old man had been helping police with their enquiries into the disappearance of Laura Page, but had been released following questioning. There were no other leads at present.

Chapter Eleven

Tuesday afternoon

Rumours fizzed out of school like lemonade out of a bottle. Laura had been stabbed, they were dragging the river for Laura, Laura had flown to Paris, Laura was living with the P.E. teacher (who happened to be absent) in a country cottage, Laura was pregnant – with twins – Laura had got AIDS. Everywhere you could hear the words 'Laura Page, Laura Page'. The words rang in my head. It was hypnotic, and I was afraid it would spin me off into the lane with the girl running, or even worse bring back the 'nothing', anything, anything, but the nothing. Deep breaths, Petra. Your Dad says you're a rock. Rocks don't get scared of anything, not even 'nothing'.

We headed for the hall and rehearsal.

'Laura Page, Laura Page, Laura Page . . .' all around us.

'SILENCE,' roared Mad Jeffers, opening the hall doors to let in the rabble.

'Pet, Pet,' hissed Seth. I tried not to listen. He pulled at my sleeve. I kicked him.

'I know who it is! I've just realised. I'll tell you later.'

'Oh, just shut up.'

'SILENCE,' roared Mad Jeffers again.

There was silence.

'I don't think she was kidnapped by the mad monster driver. So what do you think's happened?' I ask Seth as we came out of school.

I'd been waiting to ask him, and at last the police had gone after interviewing lots of people and interrupting several classes, to the annoyance of the teachers and Mad Jeffers in particular. They came into our class, but only asked us if we knew Laura Page and had we seen her on that day. They did seem to be thinking that something had happened to her, that she hadn't just run away. By now her photograph and description were in the newspapers and Mr and Mrs Page had appeared on television, Mrs Page in tears begging for her return and Mr Page asking for information, please, please. But as they went round the school I thought the police were getting anxious.

Unlike Seth, who said:

'Ah, Little Pet. I'm not going to tell you yet. But I'm pretty sure.'

'Well, shall you tell the police?'

'Of course not. We need evidence, Little Pet. But I think I can find some.'

If I'd got to put up with being called Little Pet, I wanted to find out what I could – not that I really thought he knew anything.

'What evidence?'

'Well, you must think it out for yourself. Or use your powers to read my mind.'

'It doesn't work like that.'

'Too bad. But I'll give you a clue. Someone who has access to lots of kids.'

'Could be anybody. How do we know we know them?'

'Gut feeling. Instinct.'

'Yeah, maybe. You could be right.'

I thought of the flashes of the girl in the lane, but I didn't say anything. What were they all about? I wanted to know – or I didn't want to know . . . whatever.

'I nearly always am right, Little Pet,' Seth said, smiling.

If there are only two suspects, I bet Seth's picking the wrong one, I thought, and then came a tap on my shoulder. Barney had turned up.

'What d'you think happened?' asked Seth.

'I bet she's gone to London with her latest boyfriend,' said Barney. 'Anyway, it's boring. Girls are always going missing. They talk to someone on the Internet and go off with some nasty old paedo aged ninety-seven who claims he's eighteen and looks like a pop idol. I'd rather have my new theorem . . .'

'What is it?'

'I'm into quantum physics and . . .'

'Oh, I thought you said "theory",' Seth interrupted. '*Theorems* are sad. *Theories* are happy.'

'I haven't *seen* anything for weeks,' I said. 'Only George . . .' I didn't want to tell Seth about the girl running up the hill, '. . . and he doesn't count.'

'Don't suppose he can. From what you say they didn't get much education in his day,' said Barney, then continued, 'What's going on here? Free entertainment or pay-to-view?'

We were walking as usual past Kate's part of the school, the senior part. But there was nothing usual about today. We were all at once surrounded by schoolkids, jostling, shouting, taunting each other, circulating round a ring of boys and girls scrapping, fighting, shouting – fists, grabs, slaps, kicks, punches, throws, hair flying and being pulled, shrieks and screams. A lot of kids, a lot of scrappers.

'It's a fight!' yelled Seth. 'I'm getting out of here!'

'Look! There's that Townie who chased us in the park. He's there.'

'I don't care who's there. C'mon, Little Pet, let's go. No way am I going to be involved in this!'

'Where's the police gone? They were here earlier!'

'Well, they're not now. Nor me. Bye, Pet, Barney.'

We didn't follow Seth disappearing into the distance as fast as possible. We were curious to see what it was all about so we kept a safe distance, shrank into a hedge and watched. It looked like Townies against Goths. Laura Page was a Goth. Was it anything to do with that? The ring in the middle had parted and I could see sister Kate and a blonde-haired Townie type girl bashing the hell out of each other.

'Is that Kate?' Barney cried.

'Yeah. Shall we go and help her?'

'We'd better. She *is* our sister.'

'Wait! Listen!'

Sirens came wailing down the street and hordes of police appeared. Teachers arrived too, including Mrs Matthews and Mad Jeffers. They'd cottoned on to what was happening.

'We can't help her now. We'd better get out of here!' said Barney.

'You're right.'

So we took off and raced towards the end of the road, Townies and Goths following, with police and teachers in pursuit trying to catch as many as possible. Just before we left the scene, I looked back to see Kate and her blonde-haired enemy grabbed and put in a police car. They hadn't managed to escape.

We arrived home to find Mum there, Dad out as usual.

'You been running or something?' she asked as we shot inside, panting.

'Just trying to find out who was the fastest of us,' I said.

'Where's Kate?' asked Mum.

'I expect she's staying late at school tonight,' I replied, not wanting to say that she'd been arrested.

'Doing what?'

'Er . . . a project, I think,' said Barney.

'I hope she's not seeing some boyfriend of hers.'

'I'm not sure she's got one at the moment.'

This seemed to satisfy Mum and she left the room to knock together our tea. Me and Barney looked at each other and whistled. Neither of us wanted to land Kate in it.

However, just as we'd finished tea the doorbell rang. We all sprang to answer it. Kate appeared, accompanied by a policewoman. Her face looked all sore and bruised and her hair was a mess. Mum took one look at her and screeched:

'What on earth have you been up to?'

'I'm afraid to inform you,' said the policewoman, 'that your daughter, along with several other pupils, was involved in a mass fight outside her school. She was one of the main participants. And she's been cautioned not to do it again.'

Mum gaped speechlessly for a moment, then she rallied.

'I see. Thank you for bringing her home. I can deal with her now.'

The policewoman left. Mum grabbed Kate round the shoulders and pulled her into the house.

'Well, young lady, what have you got to say for yourself?'

'It was a big Goth and Townie fight. It wasn't just her . . .' I interrupted.

'Let her speak for herself. Well, Kate?'

Kate hesitated for a moment, then she started,

'Well, we had the police round today asking about the missing girl . . .'

'Laura Page,' interrupted Barney.

'Be quiet. Carry on, Kate.'

'. . . and after they'd gone some of those Townie girls in my class started saying nasty things about her. One of them, Tracey, said that was one less Gothic slag to worry about and she wished it would happen to more of us.'

'Us? You're not a Goth, are you?'

'No, but I'm more of a Goth than a Townie. Laura was a friend of mine and I didn't like what they were saying about her. So I told Tracey to take it back and say sorry, but she wouldn't. Then I'd just left school when she came right up to me and said in my face that she hoped Laura would turn up dead. So I pushed her away and told her not to be so evil, then she hit me back and others started fighting and it just accelerated from there . . .'

'I know that's a terrible thing for anyone to say, but you shouldn't have taken any notice of her. Kate, I thought you were my sensible daughter!'

Mum sat down and buried her face in her hands.

'I just don't know what I'm going to do with you all. I feel I'm all alone to cope with everything. Your dad's never here and when he is he seems somehow . . . distant. He's been a bit strange since that girl disappeared.'

'How do you mean?' I asked. 'Strange?' Dad couldn't be connected with that girl somehow, could he? Not my Dad. Dad was special. My friend. No, no, don't think in that direction.

'Well, he doesn't talk to me like he used to. Seems miles away most of the time.'

'P'raps he's got a lot on his mind,' said Barney.

'Thank you, Barney. I'd never have guessed that myself.'

Then the doorbell rang again.

'Who is it this time?' sighed Mum. 'Kate, go and get yourself cleaned up.'

It was Seth, looking handsome and smiley and cheerful as usual.

'Hiya,' he beamed. 'Kate, it's you I've come to see. You knew Laura, didn't you? Perhaps you could help me with an idea I've got . . .' He broke off as he saw her. 'Have you been fighting . . .'

'Seth, just go away!'

'All right, all right. I can see this is a bad time. Bye, folks. See you later.'

I watched as he disappeared down the drive just as quickly as he had from the fighting earlier.

Chapter Twelve

Wednesday morning

I awoke and tried to stretch but PuddyCat lay like a ton weight on my legs. I pushed. Angrily. I didn't want to get up and go to school after the fight and trouble yesterday. Everything seemed crazy. Laura Page missing, mad fights outside school and Kate being taken off in a police van, Dad and Mum angry and the teachers at school.

One more heave and PuddyCat would be off the bed and me too, but a black flash shot into my left eye – oh no. I closed my eyes and lay still, pretending I wasn't there, that I was Barney or anyone else at all rather than open them to find a black flash at the corner of my left eye. I kept my eyes closed as long as I could and then opened them to a black flash at the corner of my right eye . . .

*

. . . the girl with the long black hair runs up the narrow twisty lane between the high banks with the
trees growing on top, her little dog on its red lead
trotting beside her. There's the sound of a car
approaching and round the corner comes a white
van. The girl presses back to where the bank curves
in a bit, her hair falling all over her face. The van
approaches her, then stops. I call out:

'Look out, look out!'

But I make no sound. No one hears me. I cannot see
her face. She presses further into the bank as the sliding
door opens. She's pinned into the space between it and
the grassy bank. She's crying out but I can't hear her.
She shrinks back into the bank. I can't hear the little
dog any more. I can see a man reaching out . . .

I must see his face. I must . . . I must . . . Then I
shall know.

Mum stood in the doorway.

'You'll be late if you don't get a move on,' she said.
'Hurry up, Petra, you'll be late for school.'

Yeah, Dad and Mum were angry – no, sad and disappointed, which was worse. Easier really if they'd
been horrible. But school made up for it. In assembly
the headteacher's lecture went on for ever and ever as
we travelled from Life's Dangers in Today's Society
to Don't Disgrace the Name of the School by Fight-

ing in the Playground and Streets. It was all true but as I listened it faded away and I saw Grandad sitting on a chair by a warm fire, reading a newspaper and looking very comfortable and suddenly I wanted to see him so much. I could hear his voice in the Old Inn that night when we'd first heard of Laura going missing, that he remembered a girl vanishing in that same lane where Laura had last been seen and where we'd nearly been killed by the Devil Machine.

As we turned to go out of the hall, I knew I had to see Grandad. Soon. Not during one of our family get-togethers. But on my own. I wanted to find out what had happened before in the past. But no Seth, Kate, Barney, Mum, Granny, etc. – just me. I could walk there after school but the days were so short now and everyone so nervous about kids being out in the dark with a killer (!!!!?) that they wouldn't let me go alone.

There was only one person who'd play it my way – that is, if I could get hold of him and if he could spare the time . . . and if I could dodge Seth, Barney and Kate.

Wednesday evening

Dad put me down at Grandad's house.

'I'll come back in an hour's time for you. I'll have dealt with the down-and-outs by then and be ready to collect the crazy. You!'

'I'm not crazy!'

'Just a faithful imitation. Have you let him know you're coming?'

'Yes. And I sneaked a bottle of beer for him. Bye, Dad. See ya.'

Grandad and me sat munching in front of the warm fire. Granny had left sandwiches and orange juice, though Grandad was drinking the beer I'd brought with me. She goes to her keep fit class on Wednesday, the last one before Christmas, so we were on our own.

'What is it you want to know?' Grandad asked. 'Is it to do with "seeing things"?'

'How did you know?' I asked.

'Well, your mother told me you didn't see things any more, but I wasn't sure – it seemed unlikely that it would stop just like that.'

'I wish it would . . .' And at last, the warmth, Grandad, the kitten (one of PuddyCat's) by the fire, did it at last, what I'd promised I wouldn't do. I cried. And cried. Me, wot never ever cries.

After a bit, he fished the paper tissues from underneath the sandwich plate and I mopped up.

'That's better. It's your great-grandmother's fault. No, that's unfair. She couldn't help it any more than you can. One thing I remember . . .'

'What was that?'

'Well, there was a whole lot of us and it was only a little cottage we lived in. And there was this wind – I can remember the noise of it even today and we were quite scared and suddenly she was in the room grabbing all of us and rushing us all downstairs and outside . . .'

' . . . And?'

' . . . the chimney blew down through the roof and all over the beds we'd been in. She'd known it was going to happen, apparently. So if it hadn't been for your great-grandmother's gift, I wouldn't be here today. Neither would your dad or you. So don't knock it, Petra!'

I'd calmed down while he was talking.

'Yeah. Grandad, can you tell me about the girl, please? The one you spoke about on your birthday night. The one in the lane?'

'I don't remember it exactly. But I think she was called Mary, Mary Linley, and she was taking the dog for a walk – it was a Saturday, I remember – and then later a boy cycling home along that lane found the little dog there whimpering. Mary had disappeared and she was never found. Everyone searched and searched, but there was no trace of her at all. That poor girl. And her family . . . they moved away, you know.'

'Do you think Laura Page is missing in the same way?'

'I don't know. I hope not. But what's worrying you, Petra? Did you know Laura very well?'

'No.'

'Then leave it to the police. And just get on with your own life.'

'I wish I could. But it won't leave me alone.'

'What do you mean, "it won't leave me alone"?'

'I keep seeing her in the lane. A girl with long dark hair. And a little dog. It must be her. And a white van comes along and stops and I try to warn her but she doesn't hear and then the picture goes.'

'Oh, Petra.'

'And I don't know if that's the girl – Mary, you said – or was it Laura Page? Did Mary have long dark hair?'

'Yes.'

'And Laura. But I can't see her face. Yet every time it comes I see a bit more of what's happening. And I don't want to. And I don't want to see his face, which I think is coming nearer each time there's a flash – and I know soon I'll see his face. Shall I go to the police, Grandad?'

'I'm not sure. You've not really *anything* to tell them that's evidence. I mean, we know there is, but will they understand?'

'I don't want them questioning me. They'll think I'm crazy. I don't like people thinking I'm crazy,

Grandad. What shall I do? And I'm not scared, but Kate's got long dark hair . . .'

'So have you . . .'

'Oh, he won't hurt me. But suppose he comes after Kate.'

'I think she's safe. Everyone's on their guard. And Petra . . .'

'Yes?'

'They're sending someone to reopen Mary Linley's case. They think Laura going missing may be connected with it and the police are fully alerted. You'll all be safe, Petra.'

'I don't want to go to the police, Grandad.'

'Look, I'll talk to your dad about this. He'll be here soon and we'll decide what you should do. Don't you worry any more. Don't be scared.'

'I'm not *scared*. I just want to know what to do. Listen, I think that's his car now.'

But it wasn't Dad. Mum had turned up with Barney and Kate in her battered old car.

'What have you been up to?' asked Kate.

Chapter Thirteen

Thursday

Our local paper, *The Chronicle*, had also discovered the fact that the vanishing of Laura Page and Mary Linley might be connected. Pictures of the two similar looking girls – both smiling and with long dark hair – appeared on the front page.

'COPYCAT SCHOOLGIRL DISAPPEARANCE?' ran the headline. Also on the front page lower down was another headline, smaller, but with a picture of Kate's rear view going into a police van:

'Vicar's Daughter In Street Brawl'

Mum went pale and sat down when she saw it. Kate sniffed miserably and promised she'd be a saint for ever and devote herself to charity and good works, but Dad said she didn't have to go over the top, just turn up at school and take whatever flak was thrown at her and keep smiling. Barney and me, we kept quiet. Part of me was sorry our paper was delivered so early in the morning, and then we might have got to school before Dad and Mum had seen it. But another part of my brain was on red alert at the photographs of the two girls – I recognised the long dark hair, though not the faces, always hidden in my flashes of the girl in the lane.

Copies of the *Chronicle* were everywhere at school. So was the buzz about the girls, kidnappings, serial killers, mystery, danger, searches, the fight, Goths, Townies, arrests, the police.

Seth appeared smiling, handsome, confident, knowing it all, anyone who'd lived in the States and Europe as he had would be familiar with all this publicity, etc. etc. He handed out his words of wisdom and homed in on us before I could escape.

'It's definitely HIM! I know it.'

'Know what?' I was playing dumb.

'Oh, I know the answer. It's got to be if both girls were at this school. He must have known both of them. You can relax now, Little Pet, the mystery will soon be solved. By *Moi*.'

'Why don't you go and tell the police, then?'

'In my own time. Never fear. Just a bit more info to gather up first. See you later. People to see, things to do.'

We watched him shoot away, full of himself.

'Bet you he's wrong,' said Barney. 'He couldn't solve a four-year-old crossword puzzle. He thought it meant you'd got four years to do it in.'

'Well, he thinks he's Sherlock Holmes.'

'Inspector Clouseau, more like,' said Barney.

I didn't see much of Seth that day, different groups. After school I waited outside the hall for choir rehearsal. He still wasn't there. Nearly everybody else was.

What's he up to? I thought. Mad Jeffers will be mad at him if he's late. Mind you, Mad Jeffers hadn't turned up yet either. The waiting crowd were getting restless.

'I've got better things to do than hang around here,' someone said.

'I'm going home soon if he doesn't turn up.'

Just then Seth sauntered into view looking like the cat who had got the cream, Jack the Lad, Seth the Superhero.

'I shouldn't wait too long if I were you,' he announced. 'Mad Jeffers has been arrested. He's talking to the police now.'

'Where? At the station?' someone asked.

'No, here. In the school. I saw the police going into his study.'

'Bet he's making it up. You can't trust him.'

'It's probably one of his tricks. I'm not going yet.'

I grabbed his sleeve and pulled him to one side.

'You told the police it was Mad Jeffers?' I asked, gobsmacked.

'Yeah. Who else could it be? Who knew both girls? I had a chat with your sister Kate. She said that Laura used to go to choir practice, but stopped. Why did she do that?'

'Maybe she just got tired of choir practice.'

'No, it's too much of a coincidence. And him knowing the other girl.'

'How do you know?'

'I asked how long he'd been here. Years and years. He's been here for ages. So he must've known the other girl.'

'You need more proof than that, Seth. I'm sure it's not him. He doesn't give off any vibes. Not the right sort.'

'You and your vibes. Who says your vibes are always right? He doesn't like me so that obviously means there's something wrong with him.'

'Just because he doesn't like you doesn't make him a child killer or whatever. You didn't really go to the police with that?'

'Well, no. I called them on my mobile. Mine's untraceable. So if there's a very small chance I'm wrong there won't be any comeback. And if I'm right

I can claim the credit for catching him. It'll look good on my CV when I join up to become a detective.'

I stood there speechless. Seth's not for real. I'd never met anyone like him before and probably never would again.

'Look. Someone's coming,' a voice called out.

Seth looked round.

'Hasn't he been arrested, then?' he asked.

'Doesn't look like it,' I replied.

It was Mad Jeffers, angrier than I'd ever seen him before. He was not good tempered at the best of times, and now his face was pale and his eyes were bulging.

'Everyone into the hall NOW!' he barked. 'I've got something to say to you all!'

When we were all in there he began, waving his rhythm stick furiously,

'Someone,' he boomed, 'and I've got a pretty good idea who . . .' His eyes gazed round the Hall and fixed on Seth' '. . . phoned the police and told them that I was the abductor. They assured me that they thought it was obviously a practical joke by a schoolboy, but that it still would have to be checked out. As a result of which I have spent the last hour having to account for my movements around the time Laura Page disappeared. They even questioned me over Mary Linley. To the huge disappointment of somebody I have been cleared. Have any of you got any-thing to say?'

Most of the class turned in the direction of Seth.

'De Freitas, was it you?' he roared.

'Me, Sir? No! Of course not,' Seth said, looking as innocent as the cherub on a Christmas card – you know they're up to wickedness, really. 'Would I do a thing like that?'

'Yes,' came a voice from the back of the class.

'Be quiet,' snarled Mad Jeffers. He'd lost his usual sarcasm. 'Right, unfortunately I have no proof or I would come down on the person responsible like a ton of bricks! Now let's get down to choir practice. And it better be the best I've ever heard, or else!'

So, in an electric atmosphere, the rehearsal com-menced. He was even more critical than usual and pounced on any mistake. Finally the torture finished and we waited outside for Mum to come and pick us up in her old banger. It was dark now.

'I was sure it was him,' Seth said to me. He looked a bit disconsolate.

'Never mind. Win some, lose some.'

'I haven't given up, though,' he said. His face brightened. 'Seth is still on the case. I can still find the culprit. I'm sure of it!'

Seth sure doesn't lack self-confidence. I wonder who'll be his next suspect? Heaven knows!

Chapter Fourteen

Nearly the end of the week, I thought, as I woke up. And what a week! It felt as if more things had happened in the last few days at school than usually happened in a whole year!

But when I arrived things were a bit less manic. The Goths and Townies in the school had been warned by the hadteacher in assembly, which seemed to have calmed them down, though they were always ready to flare up at any moment. Even Seth didn't seem to have any great new idea or scheme today. Good! I could use a bit of peace and quiet, especially since I had my own demons to cope with. George, for one, though he doesn't often appear in school.

But suddenly there he was in the classroom, in history when we were studying Victorian times, his time, I guess. I hoped no one else saw him as his agi-

97

tated face kept appearing in front of me, finger jabbing wildly. But I don't think anyone else could see
him. He was my own private demon. Go away, I
hissed in my head. I hated it when he turned up in
school. Whatever you're trying to tell me, George, do
it later. I can't concentrate with you hassling me.

Just before the lunch hour he vanished, but he was
back with a vengeance in an after-lunch literacy hour
with my least favourite teacher, Mrs Matthews. Seth
might not like Mad Jeffers, but I preferred him to her.
I hadn't seen George as much as usual recently, but
he was making up for it today. His funny old face
was almost in mine now. I tried to look past it to see
what it was he wanted me to see. A big store room?
A cellar? Yes, I've seen this place of yours. What do
you want me to do about it? Now clear off and leave
me in peace!

He did. Clear off. I could see Seth reading out loud
his latest masterpiece. Mrs Matthews stood there
with a rapturous look on her face. Seth was the apple
of her eye, her darling, her golden boy. She adored
him. She definitely didn't adore me, not that I wanted her to.

Then Seth's face faded away and George's reap-
peared. I didn't think I could stand much more of this.

'Oh, get lost!' I shouted out loud this time, acci-
dentally. George vanished, whoomph, and in his

place was Mrs Matthews and the rest of the class staring at me, Seth gasping open-mouthed. He'd finished his reading. Silence. Everyone watching me. Oh, no!

'What . . . what did you say, Petra?' gasped Mrs Matthews. 'Nothing, Mrs Matthews.'

'Yes, you did. I asked you if you'd finished your essay and you practically swore at me. I heard it distinctly. So did the rest of the class.'

The rest of the class were now all grinning their heads off.

I looked down at my empty piece of paper. Thanks to George, I hadn't managed to write a single thing. Mrs Matthews came over and together we stared at the beastly page, blank and bare.

'I thought so. Right, then, Petra, you can stay behind in detention tonight and you won't be going home until it's finished.'

'Yes, Mrs Matthews,' I groaned. Next thing, she'd start telling me to be more like Seth. If she did, I'd start screaming. But she didn't. Nobody spoke to me. Except Seth. Sometimes I think he's my friend, after all.

At least George didn't appear again that day. Too late, the damage had already been done. I scribbled my essay in detention along with a few other sinners. Mrs Matthews took a look at it, said she wasn't satisfied and I'd have to add some more. 'Use your imagination,' she cried. 'Petra – you lack imagination. You must try harder.' By the time she'd accepted it, we were the only two left.

She got up and strode out of the classroom. I followed slowly. The school was dark by now. I hoped that someone would've turned up to pick me up. Barney or Kate must've told them I'd be late. But no one was there. I wasn't allowed to have a mobile, naturally. Life just wasn't fair. I didn't want to walk home alone in the dark.

I went down the corridor and was just about to leave the building when my vibometer started shrieking 'Red Alert, Red Alert!' Oh, please, please, please just let me leave school and go home. I'd had enough of it this week to last an eternity of nothingness. Thank goodness it was nearly the Christmas holidays. What was wrong? Something was!

I looked out of the school and knew why.

Gareth was walking across the playground towards the main door.

I rushed back into the corridor, terrified. What was he doing here? Why was he at the school? As far as I knew he had no children, so why was he here? Was he after another child to kidnap or even . . . kill perhaps? I hadn't thought of that before, but

I did now. Everyone else seemed to like him, but I didn't. He scared me witless. He was terrifying. If he found me here, what would he do to me? I shot back into the classroom as he entered the building. I could hear his footsteps walking up the corridor. There only seemed to be me and him left in the empty school. Where was everybody? The cleaners? The caretaker? I was alone in an empty building with a man I was afraid of, who might be the killer. Oh, go away, please. My heart was pounding so hard in my chest it made me feel like I couldn't breathe. George, George, you got me into this mess. Where are you now? Dad once said you might be my guardian angel. They needn't have white robes and wings and haloes. So if you are my angel, *where are you* now? Please rescue me.

Was he going to come in the classroom? I looked round desperately. There was a cupboard in the corner full of books and equipment. I dived into it, closed the door and peered out through the keyhole. Books and spiky things stuck in my back. It was hell, horrible. Then he walked into the classroom. I could see him as he strode over to the teacher's desk and had a look through the drawers. Then he went round the room, looking at everything. Don't come to the cupboard, please. Could he hear me breathing? My heart beating, phlong, phlong, phlong? Did I smell? Will he sniff me out? Will he know? Know I'm hiding here. No! No! He'd kill me if he found me here. I was sure of it. George, George, you useless git, frighten him off.

But he didn't look in the cupboard. He turned and went out of the room and his footsteps grew fainter as he walked up the corridor, sounding like the steps of doom, but at last they faded away. I waited for a couple of minutes, opened the cupboard, went to the door of the classroom and looked out. No sign. I pulled open the door and raced for the main entrance like a bat out of hell, an Olympic sprinter, a gazelle on the Serengeti plain. I'd got to get out of the school. With my heart banging, I got to the main door. Escape! Safety!

Crash! I was just about to go out of the main door when I ran into someone. Was it him? Oh, no! If it was he's got me. I closed my eyes and waited for oblivion.

'Petra, are you all right?'

I opened them to see it was Mum.

'Barney told me you were late so I came to collect you. You look terrified. Anything you've . . . seen?'

'No, Mum. Only Gareth. He was here.'

'I haven't seen him. Why would he be here? Are you sure you didn't imagine him?'

'I don't know. Oh, Mum, just let's go home. Dear Mum.'

I threw my arms round her. She went pink and astonished, hugging me back.

'You don't often do that,' she said, smiling.

I hugged her even tighter.

Chapter Fifteen

Saturday

No dreams. No sleepwalking. I slept with and like PuddyCat, and when I came to it was late morning. Not that that mattered 'cos it was Saturday, Saturday, lovely, lovely Saturday, then Sunday. Two days off. Great!

Downstairs Barney was tucking into a packet of Ricicles, his favourite. Mum and Dad had already gone out – Dad on church business, Mum shopping, said Kate, in the living room watching Saturday morning television. I'll join her when I've had my breako, I thought, doing myself some peanut butter toast. I'm gonna chill out today. Take it easy. Relax. No George, no Seth, no fears, no terror (I hope). Like run up to Christmas time.

But just as I'd finished my breakfast the doorbell rang, over and over again, very loudly. I opened the

door to find Seth standing there. But he wasn't looking his usual self – he was sporting a big black eye, a
shiner. Seth? Black eye? Had a fight? He never fought
anyone. It was against his nature. He didn't believe in
fighting.

'Let me in, Little Pet. I've got to get away from my
folks today. They're having a right barney.' He then
saw Barney, who'd appeared. 'Sorry, Barney. Didn't
mean you. No, they've been having a row. Horrific.'

'Come in, Seth,' I said. Goodbye, peaceful day, I
thought. I'd need a desert island for that. 'What's
happened?'

'Mum said he'd been seeing other women. He kept
saying he hadn't, she didn't believe him and it just got
worse. I thought he was going to start hitting her so
I got in the way . . .'

' . . . and got hit instead. Brave Seth!' I cried.

'My hero,' said Barney, making toast.

'Then he started having a go at me. Said he could-
n't stand the sight of me and wished he'd got a nice
daughter instead . . .' He stopped short. 'Hey, that
gives me an idea. Suppose, suppose *he's* the one who
kidnapped Laura Page. I've never liked him, you
know. Hate him, in fact.'

I sighed. 'We're not going to start on that stuff
today, are we?'

'What happened to your real dad?' asked Barney.

'You never told us.'

'Oh, he went off with another woman. He's one of those. Haven't seen him for ages.'

Like you, Seth, I thought. I didn't somehow think Seth would be true and faithful when he was grown-up.

'And another thing,' Seth continued, 'my horrible stepfather was out on the night when Laura Page disappeared. I remember him coming in late after the party.'

'Seth, half the people living in this town probably came in late and could be suspects. We probably don't even know who.'

'But I think we do. I feel it in my bones. You must do too, with your sixth sense, Little Pet. Who do you think did it, then?'

I hesitated, then thought, why not? Why always keep it to myself?

'I don't trust Gareth,' I muttered at last.

Seth and Barney looked at each other.

'But he's a nice bloke. Why him?' asked Seth.

'I caught him snooping round school yesterday looking suspicious.'

'Loads of people go round schools. Doesn't mean they abduct kids.'

'Doesn't mean your stepdad's one either just 'cos he hit you.'

Seth then turned to Barney.

'What about you, Barney? Got any ideas?'

'I told you before. She met someone off the Internet and they went off together.'

'Don't believe it. Try again.'

' P'raps a bunch of Townies kidnapped her.'

'Bit unlikely, isn't it? Much more likely to be a grown-up. Try again.'

'I dunno. P'raps the Man in the Moon came down in a UFO and snatched her away to an alien planet!'

'Now you're being silly. Try again.'

Barney scratched his head irritably.

'Boring Uncle Baz,' he said, at last.

'Boring Uncle Baz,' I repeated. 'Why him? He's only interested in collecting things. Cards, coins, train tickets, stamps, you name it. And booze, of course.'

'Even leaves,' said Seth. 'He had a scrapbook full of them. Showed them in the pub once, boring everybody to death. What made you think of him?'

'Dunno. He just came into my head. 'Cos he's so unlikely and boring.'

Kate, cross and battered, came into the kitchen. She had a shiner to match Seth's. If someone came round they'd think that they'd been fighting.

'Haven't you lot got anything better to do than sit around talking about people being kidnappers? Laura Page was a friend of mine and nobody knows what happened to her. It's horrible and I think you're all sick!'

She stormed out leaving us looking at each other.

'She's right,' said Seth. 'What are we mucking about at? It's Saturday, for Pete's sake . . .'

That was my Dad's joke, the thing he said to me. And, I thought, I hope he hasn't got anything to do with it. We hadn't mentioned him, but Mum said he'd been strange recently. Don't be daft. Just as likely to be the Angel Gabriel as Dad.

' . . . sorry, Pet's sake,' Seth continued. 'Let's go up town, enjoy ourselves, buy some Christmas cards, CDs, look for prezzies. Why are we hanging round here?'

'Good idea,' I said.

'Yeah. Let's go,' said Barney.

'Before we go,' added Seth, 'have you got a bit of cucumber or steak?'

'Dunno. What for?'

'My eye. I've heard it stops it swelling up too much.'

Saturday night

Unlike the night before, I couldn't get off to sleep, just lay there tossing and turning. PuddyCat got fed up and jumped off the bed. I looked at the clock.

Quarter past one. My mouth was dry and I felt hungry, so I walked downstairs. The living room light was on. Mum and Dad were still up talking. I stopped to listen. They didn't see me.

'Tom, are you going to tell me what's wrong? You've been very odd since that girl disappeared. Have you had anything to do with it or do you know something?'

Dad hesitated before replying,

'I don't know anything about the latest case with Laura Page, but I do know something about Mary Linley.'

'Well, have you told the police, then?'

'I can't. It was told to me in confession. It's against my oath to betray that confession. And I've got no evidence. I wasn't told where the body was buried and if I told the police he'd deny everything. I was told that it was an accident and that it would never happen again. But then this girl Laura Page disappears in similar circumstances. What am I to think? What am I to do, Annette?'

'But who is it?'

'I can't tell you that.'

'But he must've done it again. You *have* to tell the police.'

'I've talked to this person and he swears from the bottom of his heart that this case is different. Someone else must have done it. I just don't know what to do. I can't prove anything. I've prayed and prayed and there's no answer.'

'Oh, poor Tom. I'm sorry if I haven't been very helpful recently.'

'It's a relief to tell you. Well, some of it, anyway. Come on, Annette. Let's go to bed.'

I could hear them moving around. I shot back up to bed, hunger forgotten, brain whirling with all this new info I'd learned. Well, at least it's not Dad. That's something. But it's someone he knows. Do I know him too?

My brain chugged and chuffed. I couldn't sleep. At last I knelt on my bed and stared up the hill to the Tower, showing up clear and magical in the moonlight. Maybe the Tower held the answer.

Chapter Sixteen

Sunday morning

'Seth's just been telling us,' beamed Aunt Cilla as Mum, Kate, Barney and me walked into the lounge of the Old Inn after church, 'how he's got that black eye.'

'We've already . . .' I began, and got a really evil don't-you-dare-say-anything look from the boy himself. It was a wonder I wasn't stretched out dead as one of PuddyCat's victims on the floor, it was that sort of look.

' . . . seen it. It's awful,' I gulped quickly. 'Poor Seth.'

'So brave, isn't he? Apparently, he tackled these two awful yobbos who were just about to rob an old lady and he stepped in and sent them packing. They ran off and he saved her, but being a hero has its price. A black eye, in this case. What did you say,

Barney dear? Don't mumble. I can never tell what Barney says, Annette. Have you thought of taking him for speech training?'

'I said "Hero Seth",' muttered Barney, just like a bulldog swallowing a wasp.

'I was saying, Mr de Freitas,' Aunt Cilla blethered on to Seth's stepdad, who'd just joined us, 'what a fine fellow your boy is turning out to be. Quite the hero. Getting so tall as well. You must be very proud of him.'

'Oh, I am, I am,' smiled Seth's stepdad. 'I'm so very proud of Seth.' The Borgias must have had smiles like that when they poisoned their enemies, I thought. I'd just been reading about the Borgia family, very nasty people.

'Happy Birthday,' said my mother and we all said, 'Happy Birthday' – well, not Seth – but the rest of us who he'd invited for a birthday celebration. So lots of folk had turned up, including us, though Dad would only be along later when he'd finished his duties. Grandad and Grandma weren't coming, but across the room I saw Bella and Gareth, both looking terrific, Bella showing her hand to everyone.

'Why's she doing that? Waving her mitt in the air like that?' Barney spluttered into his coke.

''Cos she's engaged, stupid. She wants to show everyone her ring.'

'Oh, whatever for?' asked Barney, but I couldn't be bothered to answer. I was trying to hide behind Kate in the corner, shielded by the heavy curtains at the leaded window 'cos I didn't want to catch Gareth's eye. Then Aunt Cilla spotted her,

'And what's happened to you? You been rescuing old ladies as well?'

'No,' laughed Bella, coming over. 'Kate's been thumbing rides with the police, haven't you?'

'Funny – both of you with black eyes!' cooed Aunt Cilla.

Poor Kate. She hadn't wanted to come out with us for she'd suffered a lot over the newspaper article and photograph.

'I thought I'd like to be famous,' she muttered. 'But it's awful. Lots of people stop me and ask questions or look down their noses at me.'

'I shall be famous,' Seth said, 'but not for being arrested. Mine will be for talent. As a singer, probably.'

I looked at Seth. He seemed to have grown even taller. Touch and go on the voice breaking at the carol service, I thought. That'll be a laugh – Seth hitting top A and missing it. Don't be so mean, I told myself. Think how disappointed Mad Jeffers'll be at his carol service being wrecked. I was glad I didn't have my solo any more. It had made me nervous –

but now, four of us were going to sing one of the carols instead.

Dad arrived, not wearing his dog collar. A lot of Mr de Freitas's and Seth's mum's friends were in the room and sometimes strangers tried to have arguments with him about him being a vicar, and blame everything wrong in the world on him.

'Shall we eat, then?' cried Seth's stepdad. The food was wonderful. Plate piled high, I tucked in till I thought I'd burst.

And Mr de Freitas was in super form. Jokes and round-the-world travel stories rolled off his tongue, wow. His ill-fated trip to China where everything went wrong had everyone laughing in stitches with him. Except Seth. He didn't care for somebody else getting all the attention. His mum wasn't laughing much, either. She'd heard them all before, I guess. I saw my dad watching them both quietly – Dad doesn't miss much. It all felt a little edgy and prickly under the laughs – how could we be having fun while all the time Mary Linley and Laura Page had vanished, perhaps for ever? When there might be a killer among us? For a moment I felt frightened and shrank behind the curtains and looked out and then . . .

Outside was a different time and it was dark. Gregorius was walking with his monks in the light from the lantern, and I watched the shadowy form of George appearing among them. They both looked up at me. No surprise. I felt very still inside. Safe. How strange that the room full of people should frighten me, but not the ghosts outside. The smell of incense was everywhere, stronger than the pub smelling of food and drink.

'Pray for us now and in the hour of our death,' sang in my head. 'Pray for the vanished girls, for Mary and Laura.'

The noise inside pulled me back into the light of the real world. There were quite a few kids and young people in the room. I noticed Seth, the centre of attention in the middle of them, laughing and waving his hands. They seemed to like him even better with his black eye. Nobody except me is thinking of those girls, I thought, but I caught Dad looking at me. He cares, I thought, he cares.

After a time people drifted away and went home till not many of us were left. Dad and Gareth, who had been talking, also stood up to go, taking care of Boring Uncle Baz, who was doolally as usual.

'Don't go,' Mr de Freitas called out. 'I'd like to show you something. Martin, you stay in charge here.' Martin's the Harley Davidson owner.

I was still thinking – what was I thinking? I don't

know, but I found I was with Seth and Barney in the back of Mum's car, following another car with yet another behind us. Full of food, I wasn't really bothering to listen to Seth, who seemed to be trying to tell me what a great person he was really, and I mustn't put him down all the time, as he could help me learn a lot about things and life and so on.

'Don't go to sleep,' he shouted in my ear.

'Yeah, belt up, then,' Barney joined in.

'Petra – listen. Wake up! We've got to have a talk.'

'Oh, no. I don't want one of your talks. Hey, where are we?'

'Going to look at something of Dad's. Some house or something – he's got ideas about it.'

I looked out of the window. We were driving up and up a narrow twisty lane with high banks on either side, trees growing at the top of them. Bare winter trees. I knew those trees. I knew that lane, that narrow twisty lane.

'Hope nothing comes,' muttered Barney, 'or we'll be smashed.'

And then I knew where we were.

'Seth! Barney! We're here. This is it! It's the Devil Monster road! That night. Remember?'

'Yes . . . of course we do.'

The lane. The flashes would come any time now. I waited. I held my breath. Nothing. No vision, no picture in my head. We drove on and up – took a left-hand turn that I hadn't seen on that stormy night. The lane went even narrower and steeper, if that were possible. Grass grew down the centre of the lane here. It wasn't much more than a track. I clutched Seth's hand, then pulled it away quickly. The steep banks seemed to bend over the road, and then we saw that in one place old rusted railings were holding back an ancient, collapsing wall. We'd come to a shabby and lonely place. Past the railings were two carved stone pillars and gates set at an angle to the road. They were open and Mr de Freitas, ahead of us, drove in. There was plenty of room for us all as we followed him.

In front of us was the most beautiful house.

Chapter Seventeen

Sunday afternoon

The wild garden dropped down, down to a valley far below full of giant trees and filled with bushes that would be covered with leaves and blossom in summer, but now were black and bare. An overgrown terraced path led down among them. I stood looking down and it was quite still.

The house itself was long and low and had once been white. Black shutters, some open, some closed, were on all the upstairs windows. The roof was of grey tiles, many of them missing. The pillars holding up the verandah were battered and chipped. The poor house had been almost broken and battered to bits, but still it stood there, holding up through storms, rain, hurricanes. Burglars and robbers had dragged all its best bits away, but it was still beautiful.

We ran down the steps of the old garden and hidden

in it we found a bricked-up well and a pool at the bottom, lying low among the tall trees. Then back up we climbed to the house itself – just us kids – the grown-ups were doing their own thing. Torn wall-paper of amazing design hung in strips off what once had been a drawing room. We trod carefully as many of the boards were rotten. Water dripped down through the kitchen roof where cupboards and cabinets were piled higgledy-piggledy and rotting away.

The others ran up the staircase with its carved banisters. 'Take care,' cried my mother. 'It's not safe.' I went to follow, but then something – a force, a wind, some power hit me in the chest and pushed me back. I remembered the hands of George and Gregorius pushing me away from the Tower. But *this* wasn't the Tower. I stood winded as the others trod upwards on the outside of the dangerous stairs. But not me. Something terrible, something wicked had happened here and it didn't want me to know.

I came out of the house on my own and looked at the outhouses, feeling very strange, for this, I knew, was a house where giant things had happened – enormous love, a terrible tragedy.

I could hear Mr de Freitas talking,

'I've been finding out about it. Dates back to 1780. Five bedrooms, attics, library, dining room, French drawing room opening on to the garden once filled with rare plants . . .'

'That's interesting,' said my father, 'but why have you brought us here?'

'Because I've bought it to restore it and I wanted you, my friends, to see it before we get to work on it as soon as possible. Maybe, my dear,' he said to Bella, 'someone as lovely as you could live in it later and make it what it once was.'

I heard Bella laugh,

'I wouldn't be able to afford this . . . It's much too grand.'

I didn't want to listen any more. I could still feel the blow on my chest telling me to stay away, this house didn't want me, that danger lurked all about us, especially me. 'I'm going back to the car,' I called out to Mum, but instead I wandered into a black and white building out at the back under the shelter of huge trees, a sort of coach house but much more grand, and as I moved on, wanting to but not wanting to, not able to keep away, I walked through the building, filled with old rubbish, looked beyond it and there it was.

The Tower. Of course, of course, of course. It had to be. There it stood, dozens of trees behind it, backing it up, sheltering it in its place above the beautiful house, above the town. I'd found it. It did exist. My Tower. Mine? Perhaps?

As if in a dream I wandered into it – only a shell of a little room now, under a pointed roof. Windows near the top lit up the four white walls and the red and blue tiled floor with its heap of old clothes and filthy blankets in the corner. A crooked walking stick lay on the floor. Shivering, but unable to stop myself, I used it to push aside the pile of stuff. There was nothing there, but underneath the tiles were broken, muddled, heaped up, some shattered into dust.

I gazed up at the roof. This was not the magical Disneyland Tower I had imagined gazing from my bedroom window. This was no Enchanted Castle. This Tower was sad, old and tired, worn out with sins.

But as I stood there I could feel a black flash coming in the corner of my left eye. Oh, no. Not today. I closed my eyes. Then I opened them to find the black flash in the corner of my right eye. It's started and I can't stop now.

A picture of a dark-haired girl suddenly appeared in front of me, very faintly, then growing clearer, then fainter again and finally disappearing, very, very slowly. And then, as the girl faded away, I could feel the nothing beginning. All sensation started to leave me, making my limbs feel numb, lifeless, everything draining away, my body, my mind, my soul, my spirit, my being. Now I could see a bright vortex of light and I began to head for it uncontrollably, inexorably, unstoppingly. I could still think, but had no control, as if my life force was ebbing away, ebbing away, ebbing away . . . The nothing was taking me into itself, making me nothing within it. Help! Help! I cried inside.

Someone appeared in front of me. Gareth! My doom! It must be him! I screamed and came back to life.

'Go away!' I yelled and power came back to every bit of me. I rushed past him, out of the Tower, past the house and garden, through the gate and down the lane on jet-propelled legs. I didn't notice whether anyone else had seen me go and I didn't care. I just knew I had to get out of that place, away from Gareth. Everything was wrong with it and him. Something evil had happened there. I never wanted to go near it again. Running out of my mind, I ran on and on and on. I reached the Old Inn but I didn't stop there. I flew on wings of flame. Running away, running away. Distance didn't matter! Nothing mattered but to escape from the Nothing! From the Tower! From Gareth! I wanted home.

I remembered that nobody was in and I hadn't got my front door key. I stopped. I know, I'll go and see Grandad and Grandma. I'd be safe with them. Calmer now, but drenched in sweat, though it was a cold day, I ran on.

*

I arrived at the welcome sight of Grandad and Grandma's house and rang the doorbell. Little barks, funny little yaps. What was going on? I didn't think they owned a dog.

Grandma opened the door and a little parcel of fur leapt up at me, licking, wagging, panting furiously. It smelt of biscuits.

'Petra, dear! Come in. We weren't expecting you!'

'Hello, Grandma. Is it yours?'

'Yes, isn't she gorgeous?'

'I didn't know you'd bought a dog. Yes, she's lovely.'

'Well, Grandad's friend Arthur's dog had some puppies recently and gave one of them to us. My, she's certainly taken to you.'

'What's she called?'

'Bonnie.'

I followed Grandma into the living room where Grandad sat by the fire. I ran and kissed him, hugging him.

'You all right, Petra? You look exhausted.'

'Well, we went to an old house. I didn't like it, so I left it to come and visit you. Oh, Grandad.'

'You're all right. Come and sit down.'

I sat down and Bonnie jumped into my lap. She was just what I needed right now, a bit of Tender Loving Care. I stroked and cuddled her, buried my face in her furriness. They watched me for a while, then Grandma said:

'Would you like her? For an early Christmas present?'

'I dunno, Grandma. She's lovely. Don't you want her?'

'Well, she's a bit energetic for us and we thought of you. Go on. I don't think your mum and mad would mind.'

'PuddyCat might,' I said. Mind you, he spends half the day lying on my bed anyway. If I kept Bonnie out of my room . . . 'Oh, thank you, thank you. She would be the best Christmas present ever!'

'Would you like to stay for tea? I'll tell your mum and dad when they get home,' said Grandma.

'Yes, please.'

I ended up giving half my tea to Bonnie as she kept jumping up at me and licking my face as I ate.

The phone rang. Grandma talked. I could hear her say I was with them and safe. Yes, safe.

But Grandad was looking at me curiously,

'What was all that about? You've got them worried stiff.'

'I didn't like the place,' I muttered.

'Do you want to tell us about it?'

I looked at the kind, wrinkly faces.

'Yeah, yeah, I will . . . when . . .'

The doorbell rang. Then Mum rushed in – she's got a key, of course – the others behind her.

'Just what are you up to?' she cried. 'You gave us a real fright! Screaming and running off.'

'She was just throwing a wobbly,' drawled Seth, coming into the hall. 'Oh, what a cool little dog . . .'

Between the yaps, the licks, the greetings, the questions, I never did actually say why I ran away.

But that night I drew my curtains without looking at the Tower. I didn't want to see it any more. I didn't want to think about it.

Chapter Eighteen

Monday morning

It was dark going to school in the morning, dark coming home at night, a world of dark. The final week before we were due to break up, so it was all Christmas chaos, cards, calendars, plays, parties, rehearsals, decorations, a sense of something in the air. And more than that, the question – what had happened to Laura Page?

Seth kept trying to find out what had happened to me in the Tower, but I wouldn't say. So did other people including my mother. My Dad said nothing, except, 'I'll wait for you to tell me when you're ready, Petra.'

Monday evening

Kate rushed into the room with news for us as we were sitting down to tea.

'Guess what I've heard? There's going to be a big fight tonight. Between the Goths and the Townies.'

I knew something had been in the air at school. Good. Compared with the disappearance of Laura Page, Goths and Townies were FUN.

'I hope you're not going to join in *this* time,' Mum said.

'Of course not. Would I be telling you if I was? I want all this stupid fighting to stop.'

'Where's this going to take place?' asked Dad.

'That's the surprise. In the churchyard.'

'How spooky!' said Barney. 'Fighting in the grave-yard!'

'Graveyards don't bother me,' I said. 'There's more scary things around than them.'

'Are you going to tell the police, Dad?' asked Kate.

'Yes. I'll have to. It sounds like trouble. When is this going to happen, Kate?'

'Around seven o'clock or just after.'

Dad left the room, heading for the phone.

'Should be nice and dark by then. Can I go and watch?' asked Barney happily. 'See the fighting and the arrests.'

'No, you can't,' snapped Mum. 'It might be dangerous. I don't want any of you mixed up in it. You gave us a big enough shock yesterday, Petra, running out of that house screaming like that. No, you're staying in tonight. And you, Kate.'

'I don't want to go and watch,' sniffed Kate. 'I told you so that it would be stopped.'

'Pity, really,' said Barney. 'I like a bit of live entertainment. Makes a change from the telly.'

'Be quiet,' said Mum. 'It's not funny at all. Your values are all wrong.'

She walked out of the room and Bonnie, the little dog, rushed in. I gave her the rest of my tea. Everyone loved her except PuddyCat who'd taken one look and shot up the big tree at the bottom of the garden where he'd spent the rest of yesterday evening glaring evilly down at me. I had to tempt him down with a tin of salmon. He didn't sleep with me last night either so I hadn't been forgiven yet. Never mind, I thought, he'll come round eventually.

Later that evening, while we were stuck inside, watching telly and hoping for news of the disappearance, the phone rang. Dad had already left for the church. Mum went to answer it. Kate was upstairs.

'I wish we could go and watch,' said Barney. 'I'm bored.'

'So am I,' I said. 'But how do we get past Mum?'

'Dunno. That's the problem.'

'It might be one of her long phone calls. One of her friends,' I said.

'It is. She's going upstairs. She always does that when she's going to have a good chat. Now's our chance.'

'C'mon. Hey, shall we take a torch?'

'Yeah. With any luck we'll be back before she's finished.'

We tiptoed to the front door. Bonnie followed us, yapping happily.

'No. It's not walkies,' said Barney.

Bonnie yapped again, louder.

'Look, we can take her with us. I'll get the lead,' I said.

'OK. But be quick.'

We shut the front door as quietly as we could and slipped out of the house. Mum, upstairs, didn't seem to notice. Below the vicarage our house and garden dropped down into the graveyard in a hollow, full of dark yew trees, the only light coming from a street lamppost and the front door of the church. We found a large gravestone and took cover behind it. I held Bonnie in my arms and cuddled her.

'Nothing's happening. Doesn't look like it's kicked off yet,' said Barney.

'Do you think we should have called Seth?' I asked.

'What for? He wouldn't come if there was a fight, the big wimp.'

'Where's the police?' I asked, shining the torch round. But there was no sign of any, no police car in the road.

'P'raps they're not here yet. Or they don't want to scare them off,' said Barney.

'Look. There's Dad in the doorway of the church.'

We could just see Dad standing there in the dim light. He seemed to be talking to somebody but we couldn't make out who.

Then Bonnie gave out a small bark.

'Shush, Bonnie. What's up?' I asked.

'Look. There's something moving behind us,' said Barney.

Down the road came an amazing sight. Goths in full gear, long black robe things, hoods, chains, necklaces, white faces, pale lips, ghosts walking through gravestones. Some carried sticks and other things, with a Big Goth leading. Some of them I recognised from our school. They came towards us. We crouched down as low as we could. It was really dark and they walked past without noticing.

'Phew,' said Barney. 'Now where's the Townies?'

Coming towards us this time, lit up by the lamplight, came a group of Townies, even more than the Goths, wearing smart casual denim gear and jackets, caps turned the wrong way round and big boots. They were tooled up as well. And leading them was the Big Townie who'd chased us in the park before.

'It's like *West Side Story*,' said Barney.

'Yeah. Who was in that film again?'

'Sharks and Jets, I think. Who's your money on?'

'Too close to call. Where are the cops?'

'P'raps they're not coming.'

The two leaders, Big Townie and Big Goth, walked up to each other to give the sign for the battle to commence. But just as it was about to start the church door suddenly opened and three policemen shot out, snarling Alsatians straining at the leashes like in a film. Shouts! Pandemonium! Chaos! as the Goths and Townies tried to flee from the police among the gravestones. Whistles, shrieks and shouts shattered the graveyard quiet. Everything was all over the place. It was hard to see exactly what was going on. A mad muddle from the look of it.

'Pity they came so soon,' said Barney. 'I'd like to have seen a bit of action first.'

'There's plenty of action going on now. Calm down, Bonnie, will you?' The little dog was trembling and shaking in my arms.

'You shouldn't have brought her,' said Barney.

'I know. But she wanted a walk. Hey, look who's coming towards us.'

It was Big Townie, who'd already dodged the police that time before from outside the school and looking like he was going to do it again.

'Let's get 'im,' said Barney.

'Him? You must be joking! He's like – massive.'

'Yeah, but we can take him by surprise.'

As Big Townie rushed past, Barney stuck out his leg, tripping him up. Big Townie went flying and landed on a gravestone, yelling in agony. A nearby policeman heard the yells and headed towards him.

'Time to split, I think,' I said. 'We don't want to get caught up in this. Mum'll do her nut.'

'OK. We've seen most of it now anyway.'

We melted away in the dark but not before I'd seen Big Townie, still yelling, being handcuffed by a policeman.

'That was fun,' said Barney.

'Yeah. Hope Mum doesn't find out.'

'She might still be on the phone. She talks for hours sometimes.'

We saw that Mum's bedroom light was still on as we walked up the road, but just as we entered the garden it went dark. She must've finished her phone call.

'What rotten luck,' said Barney. 'Two minutes earlier and we'd have been OK.'

'What are we gonna do?'

Just then Bonnie spotted PuddyCat and started barking. She rushed towards the bottom of the garden where PuddyCat had shot back into the tree and begun sulking again.

Mum came to the front door. We hid behind a bush.

'Have they left you outside then, Bonnie? Come on. Time to come in.'

She walked past us down the garden. Now's our chance.

'C' mon. Quick,' I said.

We zoomed into the house. By the time Mum came in carrying Bonnie we were back in our chairs watching television. She came in and smiled at us.

'I'm glad you've been good children tonight,' she said. We sat there and grinned at each other. I gave the little dog a special hug.

'Good dog,' I whispered. 'That was neat.'

Training Bonnie, getting ready for Christmas, trying to look pretty like Kate. That's what I want. That'll be my life, I decided.

Chapter Nineteen

Tuesday morning

School was buzzing with news of the Townies versus Goths fight in the graveyard. Both Big Goth and Big Townie had been arrested and questions were being asked as to how the police had managed to get on the scene so quickly. Someone must've warned 'em what was going to happen, it was rumoured. Me and Barney, we kept quiet. No one had seen us last night and so we weren't suspected. I didn't know whether Kate was or not and she didn't say anything. The two leaders gone, most of the sting had been taken out of the situation and all was fairly quiet. But then came news which completely overshadowed last night's events – LAURA PAGE HAD BEEN FOUND! SAFE AND SOUND!

Someone listening to the radio at breaktime had heard the news headlines and word had spread like wildfire throughout the school. So at lunchtime everyone turned on their radios, looked on the school computers or found out from someone else. The television set in the L.T. room was turned on and the room was crammed with pupils and teachers alike, everyone wanting to know what had happened. I wriggled in with Barney and Seth to catch the one o'clock headlines.

'Missing schoolgirl Laura Page has been found alive and well. She had been camping in the Scottish Highlands with a forty-year-old man, Darius Guppy, a computer salesman. He is now in custody being charged with the offence of abducting and having a relationship with a minor. It is not clear yet whether Laura Page will face any charges. She is now reunited with her parents who will be making a statement later. It is understood that she and Darius Guppy met in an Internet chatroom and their relationship started from there. The parents are believed to have been unaware of the affair.'

We waited until the news changed to other matters, then walked out into the playground.

'Wow! That's a turn-up for the books,' said Seth.

He looked staggered. He'd been sure she was dead.

'Aren't you pleased? I am! I'm sure Kate's delighted,' I said. I thought of going to have a word with her, but she was over the other part of the school and I'd see her tonight.

'Course I'm pleased. Just surprised, that's all.'

'I never thought anything had happened to her anyway,' said Barney. 'Remember? I said I'd thought she'd gone off with someone on the Internet.'

'All right, clever boy. You just had a lucky guess, that's all,' said Seth.

'Who found her?' I asked. I'd missed that bit.

'Another camper spotted her and recognised her from her picture in the paper,' said Seth.

'I wonder if she was going to come home or stay with him?' I asked.

'Who knows?' Barney shrugged. 'Why don't you ask her when she comes back to school?'

'Kate'll ask her, I expect. I don't know her. Do you think they were in love, Laura and this Darius Guppy?'

'He's just a dirty old man,' said Seth.

'I can see you doing something like that one day,' said Barney. 'Hey, it means all your theories about your stepdad and Jeffers were wrong.'

'Were they? What about the first girl? She hasn't turned up, has she? You all forgotten about her?'

I had, actually, in all the uproar caused by the Laura Page news. Poor Mary Linley. People at school didn't care in the same way about her 'cos they never knew her. Well, the pupils anyway. She was the past, she was gone.

'You can't blame your stepdad for Mary's disappearance,' I said. 'He didn't even live here six years ago. He was in America or somewhere, then.'

Seth thought about this, then shrugged his shoulders.

'You wanted it to be him, didn't you?' said Barney.

'Yeah. I hate him. I wish Mum had never met him.'

'Well, perhaps things'll start getting back to normal now that Laura's been found,' I said.

And perhaps I'd start having fewer visions and dreams from now on. I'd always had them, but not this often.

'I'm still thinking of becoming a detective, though,' Seth said. 'Well, it's one of my options under consideration.'

'OK. I'll buy you a big magnifying glass for Christmas,' said Barney.

Monday evening

Hap, hap, hap, happy talk at home. Everything was OK. Kate was singing and saying that she was going to go and try to see Laura as soon as possible. Dad looked years younger. So did Mum. Sad about Mary Linley but . . . that was in the past. Laura Page was back with us. Alive. We could all relax, Mum said.

That night I was just about to go to sleep when the face of George appeared, agitated and beseeching. I propped myself on one elbow.

'It's OK, George. She's been found. Everything's all right. She's back,' I said.

But he continued hovering and twisting his cap so I put a CD on and shut my eyes to hide his face until he finally went and I fell asleep. I didn't look for the Tower. I didn't even want to think about it and how I'd gone crazy there.

Chapter Twenty

Wednesday morning

The moment we stepped into school we heard on the jungle radio that Laura Page was returning. By now she was our local celebrity, having appeared on all the TV channels. Our crowd didn't see her straightaway because she was in the other part of the school, but we were going to try and see her at breaktime. Seth wasn't interested, though.

'Lot of fuss about nothing. Anyone would think she was a pop star or royalty,' he said. 'All she did was run away from home and create anguish.'

'Well, we're going even if you don't want to,' I said.

'Please yourself, Little Pet.'

'I bet she'll write about it in the papers and make a million,' said Barney.

'Wouldn't surprise me,' sniffed Seth. 'Plenty of talentless nobodies around today.'

'You're jealous,' I laughed.

'I'm not jealous, you idiot. Just bored!'

So, at breaktime plenty of our year went across to take a look at the famous girl. Laura walked across the playground, smiling, looking like Queen Goth amongst her admiring followers, though her smile was wiped off when a teacher told her that the head-teacher wished to see her. There were lots of different opinions. Most were glad she was back, but a few thought the same way as Seth.

'Typical Gothic behaviour,' sneered a Townie girl. 'All that pain she must've put her parents through . . .'

'You wouldn't catch US behaving like that!'

Whatever the rights and wrongs of what Laura Page had done, she'd put our school on the map. Made us FAMOUS, I thought, seeing the news cameramen and reporters at the school gate.

Long lectures from everyone about the dangers of chat rooms, etc.

Wednesday afternoon

We finished early because there was a final rehearsal for the carol concert – at the cathedral this time – to make sure of the right places and the right programme order. It was going to be a big affair and Mad Jeffers was like popcorn in a frying pan, leaping around with his rhythm stick waving in the air. The only singer he didn't criticise was Seth, maybe because he didn't make any mistakes – singing like the angel he isn't – or maybe he didn't want to have a row with him before the concert, though I guessed he'd try to get his own back later, for I bet he knew it was Seth who reported him to the police. At the end of the rehearsal we went straight home, instead of to school.

Bonnie leapt all over me, licks, barks, jumps, the smell of biscuit.

'Hi, Petra,' yelled Dad from the kitchen. 'I've got something for you.'

'Oh, what is it? Gimme, gimme. Please!' I ran into the kitchen.

'You know the old lady, Mrs Fitzsimmon, round the corner?'

'One of your fan club, yes, Dad?'

'You could say so, though I'd rather you didn't. Well, she saw you with Bonnie and thought how nice you looked and she's bought a new lead for both of you. I don't know which one of you will wear it!'

'Dad! Leave off! Here, I'll put it on Bonnie, if you keep still for one minute. It's a lovely posh lead. Oh, thank you.'

'Thank you. She thought you'd like red.'

'Yeah, I do.' For a moment a thought came into my

head, but I pushed it away. No, not that. After all, Laura Page was home safe – a scam, Seth called it, whatever that is. No one was kidnapped and I'd probably, I hoped, never, never, never see that girl with the long dark hair running up the hill again, keep fingers crossed. In fact, I was going to try to be a more ordinary girl now, I thought, walking along the pavement with Bonnie, trying to get her to walk to heel (ha, ha, she'd no idea at all). I was planning to be more like Kate, nail varnish, pretty outfits, balcony boobs – maybe lipstick, earrings, yes, that was happening at last to me, maybe, maybe, maybe being a girl wasn't too awful. Maybe. After all, like Seth's voice will break soon, I'll get my periods and, at last, Mum told me, perhaps I wouldn't see things any more. No more George, hooray. Sorry, George. No more girls running up hills, no more visions of disasters in Africa and Asia. I think I'll ask Mum if I can have my ears pierced. Bet she says no. But that's the idea. Get with it, Petra.

Bonnie pulled me along. She was going to need a lot of training. Seth's got ideas on how to do it properly, he says. We ran along the pavement past the houses, into the dip and past the church and the churchyard where the dropouts dump their bottles and the Goths and Townies have their battles, past the Old Inn, wonder if Seth's home yet, but don't stop. Bonnie was tugging me up the hill now, very happy. The sky was still blue though it would soon be dark. Past the houses.

'Let's go on a bit further, Bonnie. It's fun,' I said to her. The road had narrowed into a twisty lane with high banks you couldn't see round, trees growing on the top of them. I was singing 'Ding Dong Merrily On High' in my head as I ran along with Bonnie. Then I practised my cathedral carol 'The Holly and the Ivy'.

And then I stopped singing for I realised where I was – in *that* lane. But it was all OK. Peaceful. I'd go back soon. But I would first go on a bit further. 'Come on, Bonnie. Let's run fast.' I knew I was in Monster Machine territory, but it didn't matter. Laura Page had come home safely. It was all OK. Safe.

I could hear a car coming. The lane's very narrow. I pulled Bonnie into the hedge. Don't want her run over. I hauled in the red lead. Pushed back the hair falling over my face . . . the red lead . . . the long dark hair falling over my face . . . long dark hair . . . long dark hair like Kate's, like Laura Page's, like Mary Linley's. Suddenly I was tired and I wanted to go home!

A horn beeped behind me. A familiar face peered out.

'Want a lift? I'll take you home. You look tired.'

143

'Yeah, thanks. Good.'

I'd be OK now. He'd take me home.

He slid the door open. We got in.

'Come on, Bonnie. Enough walkies for today.'

'Had a nice day?' he asked.

'OK. But I'll be looking forward to Christmas.'

'Lots of prezzies, eh?'

'Mm.'

'Nice little dog. They told me you'd been given one.'

'Yes, she's lovely.'

We drove on. I didn't know what to say. I'd never known much what to say to him.

'You said you'd take me home. Are you going to turn round?'

'Can't yet. Lane's too narrow. I'll have to take you to the top and come back down.'

'I thought you had a red car. I didn't know you had a white van. Is it new?'

'Yes. I haven't had it for long.'

White van? White van?

And then I knew. Oh, how thick I was – how stupid! Seth always said I was stupid. I began to remember . . . a black spot started in my left eye followed by the right . . . dark-haired girl running up the lane . . . with a little dog . . . white van pulls in . . . door slides open . . . that picture wasn't about Mary Linley.

I WAS THE GIRL IN THE LANE! Not Mary, not

Laura. I'd always been the girl in the lane. Oh, no. It was about me. I was seeing the future. *That's* what George and the monks were trying to tell me, warn me. I looked across at the driver. He looked back at me.

'Are you all right?' he asked.

I was frozen. I couldn't speak. A rather sad look crossed his face.

'You know, don't you?' he said. 'I was worried about that on Sunday when we visited the old house and you went crazy in the old Tower. I was there, remember? And your mum said that you were psychic and could see things. Did you see what had happened there?'

'Let me out!' I banged at the door. It wouldn't slide across or budge. I was trapped.

'I've locked it. Look, I don't want to hurt you. I just want to talk.'

'You told my dad, didn't you?'

'How did you know? Yes, I told him what happened, but not all the details.'

'You're not going to take me home, are you?'

'Afraid not.'

We were speeding along now, going up a steep hill in a narrow lane. Then I realised where we were going.

'I'm not going back there!' I yelled. Bonnie jumped

around and scrabbled in the rear of the van. She could sense something was wrong.

What was I going to do? I thought desperately. Why did my sixth sense or whatever let me down? Why didn't his aura warn me? Perhaps he didn't have one. Some people didn't. What use had my 'gift' been to me? It hadn't warned me. He was the last person I'd suspected. I had got to do something. But what?

We'd arrived at the top of the hill with the beautiful ruined house. The gates were still open from when we visited the other day. He drove up the drive and stopped the van. Terror hit me as I saw the old Tower. No, no, no, no, no. Not here.

He sighed, 'I've always liked you. More than the others. If you behave and don't try and run away I won't make you go there,' he said. 'Now I'm going to tell you a story.'

'I don't want to hear it!' I shouted.

'No point in yelling. Hardly anyone ever comes here. Beats me why de Freitas wants this old place. No taste, some people.'

'You killed that girl in the Tower, didn't you? Are you going to kill me too?' I whispered.

'That depends,' he said. 'Are you going to sit still and listen?'

'Have I got any choice?'

'Not a lot. Anyway, here's what happened. Six

years ago, I was driving along that same stretch of road where you were walking today. It was pouring with rain and I could see this young girl walking along looking drenched. As I passed her, she stuck out her thumb as though she wanted a lift. I stopped and asked her where she was going and offered her a lift home. She gladly accepted.'

He was saying this in a completely flat tone like one of those boring lectures at school, summarising the causes of a disaster.

'She told me that she'd missed the bus and had to get home soon. We started chatting and I told her my name and what I did and she told me things about herself. She was called Mary Linley. She seemed very nice. She said how kind I was to give her a lift.'

'What happened next?' I asked, for I had to know.

'We were driving up this lane just past this old house when my car's engine suddenly cut out. It was an old car and the hill must've been too much for it. I had to get out in the pouring rain to fiddle with it. When I'd finished fixing it and managed to get it started again, I was soaking wet. When I got back in she said how sorry she was to put me to all this trouble and gave me a peck on the cheek. I was touched, gave her a hug and tried to return the kiss, but she moved her head and I caught her full on the lips. She got it all wrong. She thought I'd meant to do that.

She screamed at me, calling me a dirty old man and got out of the car. She said she knew my name and was going to tell people about me. She stormed off, saying that she'd make her own way home. I got out as well, begging her that I hadn't meant it, it was a misunderstanding. She ran into that old house telling me to leave her alone.'

'And did you?' I asked.

'No. I followed her and she ran into the old Tower. I knew the place couldn't be her home. It was still a right mess back then. I didn't think a tramp would want to live there. I pleaded with her not to say anything. I even offered her money. She refused and screamed at me. I told her to stop. She wouldn't and I put my hand over her mouth. She kept struggling and then she was still. I thought she'd just fainted. I tried to bring her round, but she wouldn't. Then I panicked, running round the place wondering what to do. I noticed there were some loose tiles in the Tower so I found an old spade in the garden, dug down a few feet and buried her, putting the tiles back. Then I drove home. Nobody saw me. There was a lot of searching for a few weeks afterwards, but nobody found her. But, then, then, I started to get these terrible dreams.'

Serves you right, I thought. I didn't speak. I was working out how to attack him, save myself.

'I had to tell someone so I told your father in the confession at the church. I told him it was an accident and I would never do anything like it again. It was a great weight off my mind, especially since after that nothing happened until the girl Laura Page disappeared. He suspected me, though I told him I had nothing to do with it. That's the whole story. If she hadn't run away this whole thing would never have been brought up.'

He paused. I waited.

'You're like your dad, y'know. Easy to tell things to. But it's a pity I had to.'

Tough, I thought. Then he seemed to come back to the here and now. His voice had been very far away when he spoke, talking like a little boy rehearsing in a play.

'Come on, Petra. It's time to go.'

'What do you mean? Where? Not to the Tower! You said I didn't have to!'

'But you do. You have to join Mary. You know too much and I can't go to prison!'

He seized my arm. I wrenched desperately, but he was stronger than he looked. He pulled me across the seat and out of the van. Bonnie jumped out and tried to bite his ankles, but he shrugged her off. I tried to kick and punch him, but it was no good. He was too powerful. He pulled me along. I was resisting every step of the way, yelling and shrieking, but nobody was around to hear. He reached the door of the Tower and hurled me in.

'Oh, no, no-o-o-o-o-oo-oo-oo!'

The face of Mary Linley appeared again, I could see her clearly. Bright lights exploded in my head. I felt drained, weak – all my strength deserting me. I hardly knew what was happening. I could feel hands round my neck, choking me, but they were only part of the whole thing. For the Nothing had come. I was lost. I couldn't talk. I couldn't speak. I was frozen, falling into a bottomless pit for ever and ever, down, down, spin, spinning, spinning, then floating, drifting into a vast grey spaceship lost in eternity in the sky. Help me, help me, don't snuff me out, don't rubbish me, let me breathe and live, let me be, I want to be, don't nothing me.

Out of the grey, nothing, lonely place where there is no warmth, no love, no hope, where I am lost for ever, a key spins towards me round and round and round. I must take that key. It's for me to take and turn, and then it will let me be – but what is it? What do you ask? The key? The key is the answer? But what is the question? Tell me. Save me. Ask me the question?

Don't come all round me, don't entrap me. Don't make me still for ever and ever and ever. Key, don't come closer, don't ask me, don't tell me that it's out there, whatever this mystery is that I must solve, oh, never, never. Please let me go. Let me out of this silence, out of this nowhere place, out of this NOTHING. I'd rather see monsters! They'd be warm, friendly, kind compared with your nothingness. Let me go! Let me go! Don't take away everything, my moving, my breathing, my living, my ME.

The Nothing has come. Nothing, please don't take away ME. Please take away the Nothing. Oh, save me. Dad, George, save me.

One scene whirls into another as whirling and blurring mists home down on me through the floating grey nothing. The key vanishes as I merge with Mary's spirit, both victims of the same man.

Chapter Twenty-one

Wednesday later

A crack was splitting the nothing and into it swirled a pale mist filling the void and out of it came George, greenish cap on greeny curls.

'What are you doing here?' I asked with my mind, for my voice couldn't speak. There he stood with his greeny curls and dreadful clothes and his sad gooseberry eyes, his hands waving round and round. Coming behind him I could hear Gregorius and the monks chanting, and smell the incense they carried. 'Pray for me now . . . Oh, no,' I cried inside. 'Don't sing in the hour of her death: please, no.' Then:

'George! Help me! Please!'

George's thin, dirty, ghostly fingers reached out for the killing hands around my throat, pulling them off me as they changed into the powerful hands of Gareth saving me, saving me.

152

He helped me to my feet and I watched, dazed, as he handcuffed Uncle Baz, Boring Uncle Baz. I must tell Barney he got it right, I thought crazily. Gareth was saying:

'Barry Grainger, you are under arrest. You are charged with the murder of Mary Linley and the attempted murder of Petra Stevens. You are not obliged to say anything, but anything you do say may be taken down and used as evidence in a court of law. Do you understand?'

'Yes,' muttered Uncle Baz.

'Gareth! You're . . . you're a policeman,' I gasped.

He smiled at me.

'Inspector Gareth Maskin of the Cold Case Squad, called in to re-investigate the disappearance of Mary Linley.' He pulled out his mobile and spoke into it. 'Bob, can you bring a team to an old house off the road from the Old Inn? You take a left turn, a right turn, go up a steep hill and you're there. Bring some searchlights and digging equipment. All right?' He closed the mobile again and turned back to Uncle Baz.

'Where's the body?' he asked.

Uncle Baz didn't reply. From far away I heard my voice saying:

'He said he'd buried her under the tiles in the Tower.'

'Thank you, Petra.'

'I don't . . . I don't have to go back in there again, do I?'

'Of course not. I'll contact your parents to come and pick you up.' He spoke into the mobile again, then: 'Don't worry, Petra. You're safe now.'

Policemen arrived and took Uncle Baz away – a little, guilty old man. Gareth wrapped me in his jacket. I couldn't stop trembling. And I couldn't stop talking.

'Funny. It was you scared me. Not him! Why were you in school that day? I thought you were after ME.'

'I didn't know you saw me. It was easier to look around when the school was empty.'

He held me tightly. It was very comforting. I knew at last why Bella loved him.

'And how did you know I was here today?'

'Don't you know another one when you meet one, Petra? When you ran out of the Tower that day I knew you'd *seen* something so we've been keeping an eye on it ever since.'

I burst into tears.

'It's a horrible tower. I hope Seth's stepdad pulls it down!'

'He probably will.' He handed me a huge police-issue handkerchief.

'Don't cry. You don't have to be scared any more. Your mum and dad are on their way.'

'I wasn't scared. You don't *understand*. It was the Nothing that scared me. It always has.'

'I do understand . . . I know about the Nothing. It's the worst thing in the world. Or out of the world. We've got the same auras, Petra.'

'I hate auras. I hate seeing things. I just want to be ordinary like Kate.'

I sobbed and sobbed. Everything hurt. My throat hurt, my head ached, my arms and legs ached, my stomach ached.

'I'm sorry, Petra . . .' Gareth began, but it didn't matter. Mum and Dad were running towards me, and behind them Barney and Kate.

'We'll take you home!' cried Mum.

My family and the forensic team had arrived together.

'No!' I cried. 'I've got to see her!'

Mum started to pull me towards the car. 'Come on, Petra love, you're in shock! You must come home now.'

'No, no. Dad! Dad! I've got to see her.'

He took hold of my hands.

'You're sure?'

'Yes. Yes. Absolutely sure. I want to see her. Or I'll think about it for ever. I have to be sure it's over.'

Dad and Mum looked at each other.

'Well, all right, if you're sure.'

'I am.'

'I want to see what they're doing,' Barney said. 'It's very interesting. I'm glad Seth's missing it all.'

Gareth was instructing the team in the Tower. As it was getting dark now they set up the big searchlight which illuminated the inside. They then got to work removing the old stone tiles and started digging. In the dim light it was eerie, weird, unreal. The white clothes of the forensic team glowed as they searched, like something from a science fiction film. Bonnie kept trying to go and dig as well and Barney had to hold her back.

After a while one of them cried:

'I've found something. Here.'

About three feet down a hand emerged, then some ribs were unearthed. And finally the skull, gleaming white despite the mud clinging to it.

'That's a child's skeleton,' said one of the group.

'I can see that,' said Gareth. He then turned to us. 'You sure you want to see any more now?'

'No, I've seen enough,' I replied. 'Yes, can we go now, please?' I tugged Dad's sleeve. 'Say a little prayer for her. Quietly, Dad. Just for her.'

Much later, back home at last, I pulled Kate up to my

room and drew the curtains across the window so I couldn't see the Tower.

'Can we swap rooms?' I asked. 'I don't want this one any more. I hate the Tower.'

'Of course. I quite fancy it here. I know, let's start tonight.'

'Wait a minute. Hang on, Kate. Oh, Kate. It's happened. It's come. My period's come.' I started to laugh. 'Just think. I'll have balcony boobs like you. But I don't want to. I'm never gonna be a girly girl! Never!'

For a moment George appeared, faint but definitely there.

'Go away!' I shrieked. 'This is private. I don't need you here just now. Even if you are my guardian angel.'

But George had already gone.

Chapter Twenty-two

Almost Christmas

They came from all over the city, all those children, for we weren't the only school taking part and the cathedral could hold many.

Everyone had said I didn't have to take part, but I wanted to. We had to sing last of all. That's because we're the best, Mad Jeffers had told us. And you'd better be the best or else, Seth de Freitas.

Seth had got all his charms together, wearing the lot.

'Do you really need all those?' I asked him. 'That Egyptian cat, f'r instance. What'll it do for you in an English cathedral?'

'You don't understand. I'll need help. You'll be there too, won't you, Little Pet?'

He'd been in a funny mood since the arrest of Boring Uncle Baz. He kept saying he was glad I'd been brave but it needn't have happened if it had all been left to him as he'd already guessed who it was. I didn't argue. I knew he was having a hard time as his mother kept threatening to leave his stepdad and he didn't want to move again. I don't want to leave you, Petra, he'd said, out of the blue. You wouldn't manage very well without me telling you what to do.

'Oh, chill out, please,' I answered, but later a girl in another class said to me: 'Aren't you lucky? You've got the best looking boy in the entire school for your boyfriend.'

'What? Seth? He's not my boyfriend. I can't stand him half the time.'

But her words stuck in my brain. Maybe, well, he's not really *gross*, is he? If I had to have a boyfriend some time it might as well be Seth, I suppose. As we took our places in the cathedral he fiddled with the charms on his bracelet.

'I couldn't sing it when I tried at home,' he muttered.

'You'll be fine. Your voice is great.'

'I'm scared it'll break on the top note – in front of all this lot.'

'You always do things well. And you're rich and gorgeous. What more do you want?'

'I'm scared it'll leave me and people'll know I'm rubbish really.'

'Oh, get happy, please, Seth. Chill out.'

The cathedral was huge – not like Dad's little church. It shone rose and gold in the candlelight, the stained glass windows glimmering with the light inside, the dark outside. There were hundreds of people there. I wasn't scared, but Seth shivered. I stared at the huge east window. There was something I had to do. I'd caught a glimpse of Mum and Dad, Barney and Kate. The other schools sang in turn. Right at the end it was us, the choir first, then my quartet singing 'The Holly and the Ivy' and at last Seth alone with 'In the Bleak Midwinter':

> What can I give him
> Poor as I am?

Seth singing of the poor? What did he know about being poor? But his voice was pure gold, in a different league from the rest. Even Mad Jeffers couldn't fault him. I was crossing my fingers on both hands.

It was over. Mad Jeffers put down his little stick and actually smiled.

When all the clapping had stopped at last and the Bishop had said thank you and a prayer, there was a silence, and it was then that I looked up at the huge east window of the cathedral with its multi-coloured stained glass windows telling the story of the world in picture after picture and at its centre the Virgin

Mary in her shimmering blue gown nursing the baby Jesus. It was then that I took the Nothing out of my mind and laid it at her feet in a silver casket. Then I sealed it all around in my mind with the lead strips they use in stained glass windows so that the Nothing would be kept locked away for ever and ever in that safe place. So I'd be free of the Nothing for ever and ever . . .

Epilogue

Daffodils bloomed in the graveyard of Dad's church, where Mary had been buried. Primroses and violets grew on her grave. I hadn't wanted to go there before now. Everything had been difficult for the family, for all of us, and it had taken time for me to forgive my father for not telling me what he knew about Mary Linley's murder. Somehow we got through Christmas. Seth helped the most, talking, making me laugh, but at last I was here. I placed the card I'd made where Mary lay and put a white rose upon it:

> I can pay you with a kiss
> From a rose on a grave.

After a time I came away. George saw me to the gate before he disappeared.